MIDDLE SCHOOL
WINTER BLUNDERLAND

JAMES PATTERSON

AND BRIAN SITTS
ILLUSTRATED BY JOMIKE TEJIDO

1 3 5 7 9 10 8 6 4 2

Young Arrow
20 Vauxhall Bridge Road
London SW1V 2SA

Young Arrow is part of the Penguin Random House group of companies
whose addresses can be found at global.penguinrandomhouse.com.

First published in the UK by Young Arrow in 2022

www.penguin.co.uk

A CIP catalogue record for this book is available from the British Library

ISBN: 978–1–529–12009–7

Printed and bound in Great Britain by Clays Ltd, Elcograf S.p.A.

The authorised representative in the EEA is Penguin Random House
Ireland, Morrison Chambers, 32 Nassau Street, Dublin D02 YH68

www.greenpenguin.co.uk

MIX
Paper from
responsible sources
FSC® C018179

Penguin Random House is committed to a
sustainable future for our business, our readers
and our planet. This book is made from Forest
Stewardship Council® certified paper.

MIDDLE SCHOOL
SCHOOL
WINTER BLUNDERLAND

CHAPTER 1

IN THE HEAT OF THE MOMENT

I'm having a meltdown!" I moaned.

I was serious. I thought I might actually be melting.

It was the hottest fall on record and (no surprise) Hills Village Middle School didn't have air conditioning. To make things worse, I was in one of the stuffiest places in the whole stuffy school building—the last row of the rehearsal room for our weekly Kazoo Khorus practice. It must've been two hundred degrees in there! The room was packed with steaming bodies and hot kazoo breath. Not a pleasant combination.

Even Miller the Killer, the toughest kid in school, looked pale and clammy.

I could smell his B.O. from two rows away. Smelled like clams. My friend Flip Savage, the funniest kid on the planet, was so overheated that his joke mojo was totally drained. Normally, kazoo practice was filled with his musical one-liners.

What do you say when a kazoo sneezes?

Kazoontite!

But that day he was slouched down so low in his chair that he was practically horizontal.

We were on the third chorus of "Bad Guy"

when the sweat on my fingers made the kazoo slip right out of my hands and clatter to the floor. The whole song dissolved into what we *musicians* call a "train wreck." Naturally, everybody looked in my direction.

"Rafe Khatchadorian!" (That's me.) "Get a grip on your kazoo! That's valuable school property!"

The music teacher, Mr. Largamente, was pointing at me with his pointy baton. He was perspiring so hard that his one remaining strand of hair drooped off his head like a string of spaghetti. He kept mopping his brow with a handkerchief but it was no use. His sweat glands were in overdrive. He had a tiny personal fan clamped to his music stand, but it was like trying to cool down a hippo with an ice cube.

I leaned down to pick my instrument up off the floor. Mr. Largamente flicked his baton. Once again, the room was filled with the sound of sixteen sizzling kazoos. That's when I felt a buzz in my pants. A new email. I pulled my phone out of my pocket and checked my screen. It was a message from Daria Deerwin, DVM—the very cool veterinarian I met at the BushyTail Animal Refuge last summer. I guess you'd call her my mentor. She taught me everything I know about wild animals—and that's a *lot*! Her daughter Penelope was pretty neat, too. She and I bonded over a bunch of lost lemurs. (Funny story—which you can read for yourself in *Middle School: It's a Zoo in Here!*)

I held the phone in my lap and pretended to play the kazoo while I read the email. Then I practically jumped out of my sticky seat. I read it twice to make sure it said what I thought it said, because Dr. Deerwin's words were like a cool breeze in a hot swamp.

Rafe—

How would you like to join me and Penelope
for a research study on polar bears in Alaska this
December? All expenses paid. Lmk if you're
interested.

Best, Dr. Deerwin

Interested? Was she kidding?! This was a chance
to hobnob with exotic creatures again! A chance to
see a part of the world I'd never seen! And best of
all, a chance to hang out with Penelope. Why did
that last thing rate "best of all"? Because Penelope
wasn't just a friend. She was totally awesome. I
can't even describe how...Never mind. If you don't
know her yet, you'll see what I mean.

I ran my slippery fingers down the screen and
tapped a one-word reply. Then, just to make sure, I
said it again and again.

"YES! YES! YES!"

Alaska, here I come!

CHAPTER 2

THE COLD SHOULDER

Over my dead body!"

That was Mom's first reaction. Quickly followed by "Out of the question!" and "Are you crazy?" and "What planet are you on??" Obviously, my polar plans had hit a snag.

One of Mom's main objections was that the trip would take me away from home over Christmas. For the first time in family history, I'd miss Grandma Dotty's Kris Kringle CookieFest and all the other classic Khatchadorian holiday traditions. Skating at the village reservoir. Caroling on the town square. Dressing up our dog, Junior, as a Christmas elf. Good times for sure.

"But, Mom," I argued, "how many times in life

do you get a chance to come face-to-face with a real polar bear in the wild?"

Wrong argument.

"Rafe, you *do* realize that polar bears have been known to eat people, right?"

"Mom! Polar bears eat *seals*!"

"Of course," she said, "that's their preferred prey. But if there are no seals handy, guess what? I'll bet a healthy middle school boy would make a pretty tasty morsel!"

I was getting nowhere. Years of life experience had taught me that Julia Khatchadorian was no pushover. And once her mind was made up, it was hard to make her budge. Clearly, I needed help building my case. I needed a brilliant presentation. A real showpiece. And I knew just the person who could help me pull it off.

Unfortunately, she was the last person in the world I wanted to ask.

CHAPTER 3

HER MAJESTY WILL
SEE YOU NOW

I asked her anyway.

As you may have heard, my kid sister, Georgia, and I have our differences. Sibling rivalry. Territorial disputes. Battles over the last Christmas cookie. All that stuff. But deep down, I have to admit that she's pretty smart—and her school projects are *legendary*. Her presentation on "Pythagorean Principles in the Design of the Great Pyramids" still has the math department buzzing.

In her entire school career, Georgia has never missed an assignment, never been late for class, never forgotten her locker combination. I think

there's already a place reserved for her in the Hills Village Alumni Wall of Honor. So I figured I'd be crazy not to take advantage of her freakishly overdeveloped brain.

When I told her about the Alaska trip, I think she was a little bit jealous. On the other hand, she kind of liked the idea of getting me out of the house for a whole two weeks over the holidays. That way, I wouldn't interfere with sleepovers and practice sessions with her all-girl rock band,

We Stink. I even told her she could use my room for equipment storage. And of course, with me away, she'd have more Christmas cookies for herself.

"Okay," she said, "I'll help you out. But it won't be a walk in the park."

Georgia had to admit that Mom had some solid objections. But nothing a great DoodlePoint presentation couldn't overcome. Georgia was the *Duchess* of DoodlePoint!

"Where do we start?" I asked.

"Research!" said Georgia. "There's no substitute for hard data."

So right after dinner, she put me to work digging up the latest stats on global warming and its effect on the arctic ice shield, the threats to Indigenous people, and the status of the Endangered Species Act. Meanwhile, she started whipping up graphs on ocean currents, Alaskan geography, and polar bear life expectancy. She made it look easy, but I know it wasn't. She was really pulling out all the stops for me.

At two in the morning, the presentation was finally done. We sat on the edge of my bed and watched it together on her laptop. It was three minutes of wall-to-wall, hard-core convincing. This was Pentagon-quality stuff. Tough to argue with.

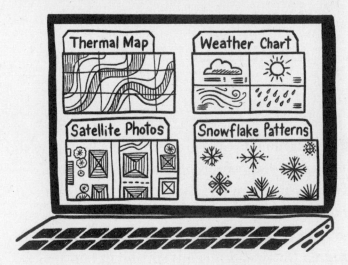

"Wow!" I said at the end. "It's *great!*"

I looked over at Georgia. She was twirling her hair the way she does when something's bugging her.

"It's close," she said. "But not perfect."

"What's missing?" I asked.

She stopped twirling her hair the way she does when she gets an idea.

"Just one little thing," she said.

CHAPTER 4

AN AUDIENCE OF ONE

The next night, Georgia set up her laptop so the presentation would play on the big screen—aka our living room TV. By the time Mom came home from her job at Swifty's Diner, the house was filled with the aroma of fresh popcorn. (My idea.) Grandma Dotty was already sitting in her favorite chair, waiting for the show to start.

"What's this?" asked Mom. "Is it movie night already?"

I escorted her to a place of honor in the middle of the sofa. I sat down next to her. Georgia sat down on the other side, with her laptop in her lap.

"Georgia and I have something to show you," I said.

"This better not be about that crazy polar bear

trip," she said. "I told you we're *done* with that discussion."

"Mom," said Georgia, "just watch."

I'd sprinkled some doggy treats under the sofa so Junior would come over and snuggle against Mom's feet. I hoped that would help soften her up.

"Let's go!" said Grandma Dotty. "I don't want to miss *The Bachelor*!"

That added a little time pressure. I dimmed the lights. Georgia lifted the lid on her laptop and pressed Play.

The title came up on the TV screen: MISSION TO THE ARCTIC: A RACE AGAINST TIME. (My title!)

For the first minute or so, the presentation was all facts and logical arguments—bullet point after bullet point on the polar ecosystem and the importance of firsthand field research, with spiffy graphics and nifty wipes.

Then the music started.

It was low volume at first, but then it started to build. Mom perked right up.

It was her favorite singer, Celine Dion. I *told* you my sister was a genius. Georgia looked over at me and winked.

When the screen showed a scene of a mama polar bear cuddling with two adorable cubs, Georgia had synced it to the lyrics from Celine's "Because You Loved Me."

You're the one who held me up
Never let me fall...

Cute little paws. Cute little snouts. Furry little faces. Accompanied by sweet violins and Queen Celine's magical voice. Grandma Dotty stopped nibbling her popcorn. I looked over at Mom. She sniffled a bit, and then I saw a little tear begin to form in the corner of one eye. She started to hum softly along with Celine, rocking back and forth on the sofa. And when the last slide faded out, she melted like a polar ice cap.

"Oh, for heaven's sake, Rafe!" she said. "If you think your research will really help those poor polar bears, then *go*! You have my blessing."

I reached behind Mom's back to give Georgia a high five. Then I pulled my phone out of my pocket and texted Penelope. In all caps.

IT'S ON!

CHAPTER 5

ALL GEARED UP

Time flies. That is, except when you can't wait for something to happen. Then time crawls—slower than a snail in a patch of bubble gum.

I spent the rest of the fall reading all the books I could find about Alaska. I devoured *Julie of the Wolves*, I raced through *Dogsong*. I loved *Diamond Willow* and *The Impossible Rescue*. I even enjoyed an oldie-but-a-goodie called *The Call of the Wild*. Really exciting stuff, and it made it even harder to wait. I thought December would never *ever* come, but finally it was here.

Packing day!

As soon as Mom gave me the green light for the trip, I'd started asking all the important questions. Would I need a passport? Nope. Would I need any shots? Nope. Would I need tanning lotion? Doubtful. Would I need any special clothing or equipment? Yes, definitely!

Fortunately, Dr. Deerwin had emailed a detailed list of items required for an average December temperature of -8°F (not counting wind chill). It's a good thing her research grant covered the cost, because this stuff got pricy! Mom and I went through the list as I laid everything out on my bed.

Down parka. Check.

Kamaak. Check.

Wool socks. Check.

Snowshoes. Check.

Ice axe. Check. (Note: Expect some questions from airport security.)

Crampons. Check.

Hand warmers. Check.

Thermal underpants. Check.

At the last minute, I decided to try everything on. When I was done, I was about twenty pounds heavier. I waddled into Mom's bedroom and checked myself out in her full-length mirror.

I thought I looked like Sir Edmund Hillary at the summit of Mount Everest. But Georgia felt something was lacking.

She ran into her room and came back with a down vest decorated with the We Stink logo. I slipped it on under my parka. I had to agree. It brought the whole outfit together.

"I hate to say it," said Georgia, "but you look kind of cool!"

After my mini–fashion show, Mom helped me stuff everything into my duffel bag. And I mean *stuff*! For a minute I didn't think it was all going to fit. In the end, I had to bounce my butt on top of the bag while Mom yanked the zipper shut. I hoped it wouldn't pop open at the airport. I hated the thought of my underpants exploding all over some poor baggage loader. When I was finished packing, Grandma Dotty handed me a little plastic bag with a red ribbon.

"Since you won't be here for my Kris Kringle CookieFest, I baked you some goodies in advance."

"Gosh, thanks, Grandma!" I said. I stuffed the cookies into my backpack, and I gave her a big hug. I would definitely miss Grandma Dotty over the holidays. She's the one who always makes sure that the tree gets trimmed and the windows get sprayed with snowflake stencils and the ugly sweater contest gets judged fairly. The holidays are her favorite time of the year, and I knew she was sad that we wouldn't all be together. I was, too.

Just before bed, I filled out my name and address on the luggage tag. I should have written smaller. All I could fit was "Rafe Khatcha." Close enough. Then it was time to get some sleep before departure day.

Fat chance.

Three hours later, my eyes were still wide open, staring at the nightglow stickers from the video game Wormhole on my ceiling. I was twitching from head to toe and my heart was thumping. When I thought about the trip, I didn't know who I was more excited about seeing. Polar bears. Or Penelope.

CHAPTER 6

TIGHT SQUEEZES

Rafe! It's b-been s-so long!"

Penelope had grown a couple of inches since the summer. When she ran up to hug me, our heads almost bumped. Awkward. She was dressed in a bright-orange parka and her braids dangled out of a blue ski cap with a red pom-pom on top.

Note 3-inch growth spurt

Penelope looked terrific. Even more terrific than I remembered. Even the way she talked was special. I admit, when I first met her, her stutter threw me for a loop. But I got used to it. And now I really liked it. It was *her*.

"It's g-great to s-see you!" she said.

"Great to see you, too!"

In fact, it was *more* than great. But it also was a little confusing. Because even though Penelope was a good friend, I realized that I kind of, sort of, *maybe* had a tiny crush on her, too.

There. I said it:

I, Rafe Khatchadorian, have a crush on Penelope Deerwin!

Of course, I could never say it out loud. And never to Penelope herself. *NeverNeverNever!* What if she didn't feel the same way? What if she thought I was some kind of stalker? All I knew is that I felt happier when I was around her. That was good enough for the moment. I didn't want to push my luck.

Dr. Deerwin was right behind Penelope, hauling all their luggage and equipment. I reached up to shake her hand, but she bent down and wrapped me up in her arms. She lifted me right off the floor like I weighed nothing.

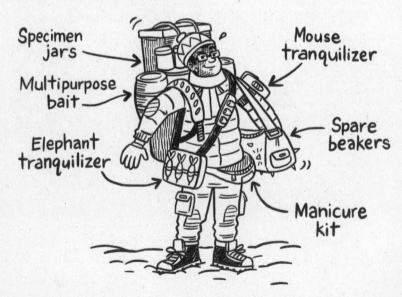

Specimen jars

Multipurpose bait

Elephant tranquilizer

Mouse tranquilizer

Spare beakers

Manicure kit

"So glad you're coming, Rafe!" she said. "It'll be great to have another animal expert along."

Dr. Deerwin was tall and fit and had great posture. To me, she looked like a real-life superhero. And to the animals she took care of, I guess she really was.

"Just got back from Borneo," she said. "Had to rescue a few sick rhinos."

That explained her midwinter tan.

While Dr. Deerwin and Penelope checked their gear at the front desk, I said my good-byes to Mom, Grandma Dotty, and Georgia. I tried to keep it light. No weeping and wailing, please.

"You owe me," said Georgia as she punched my arm. And I did. Without her DoodlePoint skills, I wouldn't be standing there.

"Stay warm. Stay safe. Listen to Dr. Deerwin," said Mom. "I love you."

"Love you, too," I said.

"Take a picture of the Northern Lights for me," said Grandma Dotty.

"I will," I said, trying not to squeeze her too hard. Grandma Dotty was so thin it felt like she might shatter into tiny pieces at any moment.

I waved good-bye as they all headed down the escalator. I felt a little burn in my throat as I watched their heads disappear over the horizon. But before I could start missing anybody, I felt Dr. Deerwin's strong hands on my shoulders, pushing me in the right direction.

"This way, Rafe!" she said. "Time to board!"

Turns out Dr. Deerwin had some kind of super-deluxe research clearance, so they whisked us through security like we were Hollywood stars. They didn't even ask about my ice axe. And just a few minutes later, we were walking up the ramp and onto the plane.

The flight was packed! Naturally, I hoped that I'd be sitting next to Penelope. That would give us six hours to catch up on life and reminisce about our days together at the BushyTail Animal Refuge. But when I showed my boarding pass to the flight attendant, he told me there'd been a little mix-up.

When Penelope sat down in row 5, the flight attendant sent me back, back, back—all the way to row 42! Smack between the two rear bathrooms. Any farther back and I'd be sitting on the tail fin.

Even worse, it was a middle seat. And even

worse than *that*, the seat was between two
lumberjack-looking dudes in flannel shirts and
industrial-strength snow pants. They were both so
bulky there was barely room for a peanut in the
middle of them. And the peanut was me.

"Yo!" they both said as I plunked down in my
seat. They probably hoped they'd have the middle
seat to themselves so they could spread out their
massive thighs. They both wore heavy boots and
had really deep voices. They kind of looked like

twins, but maybe that was just the matching plaid.

"So," I said, "you're heading to Alaska, too? The Frozen North! The Last Frontier!"

"Yup!" said the dude on my right.

"We're Iditarod racers!" said Left Dude.

"The *Iditarod*? You mean the big dog sled race?" (Yep. I'd done my Alaska homework.)

"That's right!" said Right Dude. "A thousand miles over the tundra, from Anchorage to Nome!"

"The race doesn't start till March," said Left Dude, "but we figured we'd get in a few practice runs with the dogs."

"We've got sixteen champion huskies in the cargo hold right now," said Right Dude.

Sixteen huskies!? No wonder these guys smelled like dog food. At least, I *prayed* it was just dog food.

CHAPTER 7

GUT WRENCHER

Good thing I didn't have to use the bathroom. Once I was in my seat, there was no way I was getting out again. During the in-flight movie, Left Dude dozed off and fell asleep on my shoulder. His beard was so close to my face that I could tell what he had for breakfast. Looked like Froot Loops. And maybe some bacon.

I tried to reach the magazine in the little seat pouch for some reading material, but my arms were pinned to my sides. The flight attendant tossed me a pack of Onion Chippies for my complimentary snack, but I could hardly reach into the bag. I felt like a prisoner being escorted to a maximum-security lockup. No need for handcuffs. The big dude double-squeeze did the job.

As the plane started to descend, the pilot came on the speaker to make an announcement in his super-friendly pilot voice:

"Ladies and gentlemen, welcome to the forty-ninth state! If you look out your window to the right or left of the aircraft, you'll see...absolutely nothing!"

He was right. We were coming in for a landing at Deadhorse, Alaska, which is about as far north as you can get and still be in America. And there was nothing below but white. No lawns. No trees. No pools. No hills. Nothing but snow. For miles and miles.

When we walked down the stairs from the plane, most of the passengers headed into the

terminal building, which looked kind of like a
cement factory. But not us. Dr. Deerwin stood by
the baggage door while they unloaded our stuff.
Then she pointed across the runway.

"There's our next flight!" she said.

Was she joking?

From a distance, the plane looked really small.
We hauled our stuff over. Up close, it *still* looked
really small. Instead of wheels on the bottom, it had
skis. And instead of jet engines, it had one sorry-
looking propeller. Looked like the kind you wind up
with a rubber band. There were no flight attendants
or baggage handlers. Just a pilot with a handlebar
mustache and a baseball cap. His name was Phil.
At least that's what it said on his cap. Phil helped
Dr. Deerwin shove our stuff into a compartment
underneath the wings, then we all climbed aboard.

The cabin of the plane was about the size of a washing machine. This time I would *definitely* be sitting close to Penelope! Maybe too close. The seats were so tight together that when I plopped myself down, I almost landed in her lap!

"T-T-Tiny, isn't it?" Penelope yelled over the sound of the engine. I nodded.

"This is the only way!" shouted Dr. Deerwin. "Where we're going, there's no airport!"

Phil pulled up the steps with a rope and gave us a thumbs-up before squeezing himself into the cockpit. He shouted a few words to the control tower on his headset, and then we started to roll down the runway. It was like being in a go-kart with wings. We bumped, we rumbled, we bounced. And then we lifted off!

I thought things might smooth out after we were in the air, but I was wrong. The plane was going up and down like a yo-yo the whole way. I could feel myself turning green and my stomach turning inside out. All of a sudden, the taste of the Onion Chippies made a return appearance in my mouth. I thought I was about to lose it. *Hold on,*

Rafe! Don't toss your chips in front of Penelope!

I concentrated on other things to distract myself. I looked out the tiny window and started counting clouds. There weren't that many. So I started to replay my whole last Wormhole tournament in my head.

I looked over at Penelope. Cool as a cucumber. Or so I thought. Looks can be deceiving. The instant the plane touched down, she leaned over and hurled her Onion Chippies all over my brand-new parka.

"S-S-Sorry, Rafe!" she said.

No problem. Better her than me. And in a way, I was glad to see that she wasn't perfect. Besides, the parka was totally washable. Mom checked.

CHAPTER 8

BRRRRRRR-ING IT ON!

When we got out of the plane, we were in the middle of nowhere. And I mean NOWHERE! Compared to this, Deadhorse looked like a thriving metropolis. I checked my watch. High noon. So how come it was so dark outside?

"Polar twilight," said Dr. Deerwin. "This time of year, the sun is so low the only light we get is *reflected* light. You'll get used to it."

I guess I didn't need to pack those wraparound shades.

Phil helped us unload our stuff, then climbed back into the cockpit. The propeller started to turn. The plane slid forward on its skis, faster and faster.

We waved to the flying washing machine as it took off. When the sound of the engine faded away, the world got very quiet. The quietest I'd ever heard.

Usually, twilight meant crickets. Maybe a few bullfrogs. Up here, there was none of that. Not a cheep. Not a peep. Not even any wind. It was so quiet it was crazy. And so empty-looking it was scary.

"It's b-b-beautiful!" said Penelope.

That's one of the things I liked best about Penelope. She was always seeing the positive in any situation. Even when things looked totally bleak.

Oh. Did I mention the cold? It's definitely worth mentioning. Because it was colder than any cold I'd ever felt in my life—times a *hundred*! *Pinkie*-freezing cold. *Hair*-freezing cold. *Snot*-freezing cold.

Lake at Camp Wannamorra

Swifty's Frozen Slushy

Ice Cube Tray

Troll Master's Heart

Northern Alaska

Dr. Deerwin put her hands on her hips, took a deep breath, and exhaled a huge cloud of steam. Nothing seemed to faze her. In fact, if there's one thing I've learned about Dr. Deerwin, it's that when conditions are tough, she gets even tougher.

Unlike me.

"What now?" I asked. I was shivering. I could feel my lips turning blue. I had my hands stuffed under my armpits, but it wasn't helping. It just meant I had cold hands and cold pits.

Dr. Deerwin walked over to a pile of snow and reached underneath. Under the snow was a thick canvas tarp. She whipped off the tarp like a magician doing a big finale. And guess what? Under the tarp was a gleaming BlizzardBuster snowmobile with two sidecars and a trailer sled!

Leather seat

Avalanche avoidance system

Snow flap

Track

Running board

"V-V-Very c-cool!" said Penelope.

"Hop aboard, kids!" said Dr. Deerwin. "The research center is a few miles north."

I slid into the left sidecar and stretched my legs out in front of me. It was like being in a little bathtub with a hood and windshield. Penelope took the right side. Dr. Deerwin hopped onto the main seat and fired up the engine. Before we started off, she handed us our helmets and ran through a list of possible dangers on our route: Frostbite. Snow pits. Hidden crevasses. Frozen creeks. Wolf traps. Wolf packs. She didn't mention an attack from the Abominable Snowman, but it seemed like a real possibility.

At that point, I admit I was having second thoughts. I couldn't feel my nose. I couldn't feel my toes. And on top of everything else, I really had to pee. But I was afraid if I did it outdoors, it might freeze midstream. Maybe I could just go in my snow pants. Would anybody really notice?

CHAPTER 9

A GUIDED MOOSILE

When Dr. Deerwin gunned the engine, my sidecar started vibrating like a bean in a blender. Then we took off across the tundra. I thought the ski-plane ride was rough, but that was *nothing* compared to this. We bumped. We rocked. We jolted. It didn't help that the ground underneath us had been frozen solid for ten thousand years. They don't call it permafrost for nothing.

After a few miles, I got used to the rough bouncing. And my eyes were finally adjusting to the polar twilight. Now everywhere I looked, I didn't just see snow and sky—I saw animals! And they were *amazing*!

We whizzed past a herd of caribou—hundreds

of them! Then we zipped by a bunch of musk oxen. They looked like a cross between a lion and a buffalo. We zoomed past a family of Dall sheep, with huge curly horns. I hadn't seen so many wild animals in one place since my days at BushyTail. And the animals out here weren't stuck in pens or artificial habitats. They were free to roam as far as they wanted.

On the negative side, they didn't seem to have much to eat besides snow. Not a very balanced diet, if you ask me. I wished I'd brought along some of Junior's dog treats. They probably would have gone over big.

I looked across the snowmobile at Penelope in the other sidecar. She had the biggest smile on her face. I've never met anybody who loved animals more than Penelope does. When she saw the caribou and the musk oxen and the sheep, I don't even think she minded the cold.

Dr. Deerwin cranked the handlebars and made a left turn. I leaned hard against the side of my sidecar. Suddenly I saw a shadow rising up from a creek bed a few yards away. A shadow with *antlers*! Holy moly, it was a *moose*! Until that very moment, the only moose I'd ever seen was in a cartoon. I couldn't believe how big it was in real life. This thing looked like a truck with fur. The antlers were so wide that my whole body could fit in the middle—*lengthwise*.

"Hey, look!" I shouted. "It's a moose!"

I think Dr. Deerwin shouted back, "It's a bull!" But I'm not sure. Because when I turned for a better look, my knee hit some kind of release lever. Suddenly, my sidecar wasn't attached to the snowmobile anymore. I was flying solo across the tundra! I was going so fast that I actually shot out in front of Dr. Deerwin and Penelope. Snow was spraying up along the sides and my windshield was getting covered in white. *Everything* was white. Which is probably why I didn't notice the snowdrift. Until I hit it.

Suddenly everything went dark.

I felt snow pouring down the collar of my parka and filling up my sidecar. I realized that I was buried *inside* the snowdrift. Pretty humiliating, and a little scary. I couldn't see anything. I couldn't hear anything. I wondered if Dr. Deerwin had noticed that she was missing a passenger. Then I saw the snow in front of my face start to move! I thought I was about to be the victim of a cave-in. Someday, in a few centuries, archaeologists would dig me out and dissect me to see what I'd eaten last. I wondered if they'd recognize Onion Chippies.

Suddenly a hole appeared in the snow in front of me. I saw Dr. Deerwin peeking in, with Penelope right beside her. They both had mini–snow shovels in their hands. I should have known that the Deerwins would be equipped for any emergency.

"R-R-Rafe! What h-h-happened?" asked Penelope.

"I'm not sure," I said. "I must have hit the wrong button!"

"That's what I get for renting a secondhand snow machine," said Dr. Deerwin.

It only took a few minutes to excavate me. Dr. Deerwin reattached my sidecar to the snowmobile. She disarmed the release switch and then, just to be safe, she tied the sidecar to the snowmobile frame with a couple of huge bungee cords.

"We've got to make up some time now!" she said as she turned on the engine. It was no longer just polar twilight. It was polar *darkness*. I thought I heard wolves howling in the distance. They sounded hungry. And if they tracked us down for supper, it would be all my fault. As usual.

It was only thirty minutes into the mission and

already I'd caused a big delay. I'd messed up in front of Dr. Deerwin, in front of Penelope, in front of the whole frozen tundra.

Somewhere, I knew a moose was laughing at me.

CHAPTER 10

WELCOME TO NOWHERE

It's not much farther!" Dr. Deerwin shouted as we sped along.

I'm not sure how she knew that. The snowmobile didn't have a GPS and she wasn't looking at her cell phone. I think Dr. Deerwin has a foolproof directional mechanism built into her brain. It's probably how she finds her way out of jungles and caves. And now it was leading us directly to our polar research complex. I could hardly wait!

Ever since I'd heard about the trip, I'd been picturing the research center in my mind. I imagined a huge bio-dome with its own self-sustaining climate and food supply, kind of like a colony on Mars.

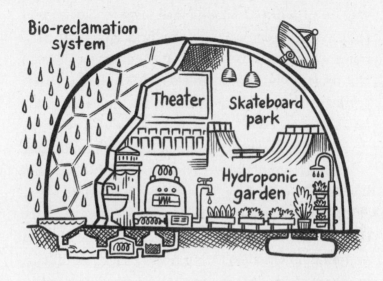

Bio-reclamation system

Theater

Skateboard park

Hydroponic garden

We'd all have our own private sleep pods and probably some treadmills and stationary cycles to keep us in tip-top shape. I hoped they'd have a satellite dish and maybe even a video game hookup so I could polish my troll-blasting skills in my spare time.

"There it is!" shouted Dr. Deerwin.

She was pointing at a little dot in the distance. I popped my head up over my windshield for a peek. Could that be it? As we got closer, we passed a wooden sign that said RESEARCH STATION ALPHA. It was hand-painted, like a class project. Not a good sign. As we drove up, I got my first look at the place where we'd be spending the next two weeks. Not a bio-dome. Not even close. More like a rusty trailer with a plastic outhouse. So much for high-level science.

Even Dr. Deerwin looked a little disappointed.

"Is th-this it?" asked Penelope. I could see that her usual bouncy spirit was a little deflated.

Dr. Deerwin parked the snowmobile. We trudged across the snow to the trailer. Dr. Deerwin pounded on the door. A big hunk of ice fell off the roof and almost hit me in the noggin. The door opened.

I expected to see a team of seasoned research scientists inside. Instead, there were just two kids about my age—a boy and a girl. From the nature documentaries I'd watched, I guessed they were Alaska Natives, probably Inuit.

They seemed to know Dr. Deerwin was coming, and they were really excited to see her.

"Welcome, Doctor!" said the boy. "I'm Panuk, and this is my sister, Uki."

Uki waved. She seemed shy.

"Nice to meet you both," said Dr. Deerwin. "Who's in charge here?"

The two kids looked at each other, then at Dr. Deerwin.

"*Uvaguk!*" said Uki. "*We* are!"

CHAPTER 11

SCIENCE ON A SHOESTRING

Once we all crammed inside the trailer to warm up, Panuk and Uki explained the situation. Apparently, the local government had cut back on science grants. Which meant the polar bear research budget had been slashed.

"Where are Dr. Pisco and Dr. Lartey?" asked Dr. Deerwin. "They're the ones who contacted me."

"They got jobs on a crab-fishing boat," said Uki. "More job security."

"Now me and Uki do everything," said Panuk. "Fix the tracking equipment, keep the logs, write down everything we see."

"D-D-Do you get paid?" asked Penelope.

"Minimum wage," said Uki. "And a weekly blubber allowance."

"Th-Th-That's c-c-cool," said Penelope.

Panuk looked at her. I knew what was going on in his brain. From the way Penelope sounded, he thought her lips were shuddering from the cold.

"Sounds like you're freezing," said Panuk. He reached for a blanket and wrapped it around Penelope's shoulders. I opened my big mouth to clear things up, but Penelope beat me to the punch.

"It's n-n-not from the c-cold," she said. "I s-s-stutter. N-No big deal. I know w-what to s-say. It j-just takes me a little l-longer to s-say it!"

I could see that Panuk liked Penelope right away.

"No problem," he said. "I understand you just fine. Keep the blanket anyway." It was a pretty spiffy blanket, thick and soft, with animal designs all over it. I have to admit, I was envious.

It also bothered me that Panuk was really good-looking, with straight black hair and dark-brown eyes. Boy-band quality. And I could tell that he had some muscles under his sweater. He probably did push-ups in the snow. Compared to him, I looked like a noodle.

While we were getting acquainted, Dr. Deerwin was looking over the science equipment in the trailer. She picked up one of the logbooks and starting running her finger down the columns.

"What's the status?" she asked.

"There are three polar bears in the area," said Panuk.

"PB1, PB2, and PB3," said Uki. "They're all coded in the logs."

"So I see," said Dr. Deerwin. "Very thorough."

Panuk and Uki looked like a couple of middle schoolers, but when it came to polar bear research, they really knew their stuff.

"The bears should all still have tracking collars from a couple years back," said Panuk, "but we haven't had a transmission from any of them in weeks."

"*Weeks?*" said Dr. Deerwin. She frowned.

"Could be our equipment," said Panuk. "It's seen better days."

He wasn't kidding. This stuff looked older than Grandma Dotty's radio. There were loose wires and cracked dials everywhere. Over in the corner was a bent aluminum antenna. This was definitely not *National Geographic* level.

It was barely local science-fair level.

And what's this about no polar bear sightings in *weeks*? That didn't sound good. How do you misplace a polar bear, let alone three of them? Did the whole species suddenly go extinct just in time for my visit? Was my elaborate DoodlePoint presentation a waste of time? Did I come all this way for nothing? Before I could worry myself into a lather, Uki invited us all to sit down and get comfortable. Apparently, it was suppertime.

"Who's hungry for *aivik*?" she asked.

CHAPTER 12

A TASTE OF EVIL

I hadn't noticed at first, but right behind the research equipment, there was a tiny stove with a steaming pot on top. Now that my nostrils were partly thawed, I could smell something cooking. Something…unusual.

We all sat down around a tiny wooden table while Uki gathered some wooden bowls. She went to the stove and started ladling out some kind of stew. Then she brought the steaming bowls over to the table, balancing them all on one arm like a waitress at Swifty's Diner. I could already see that Uki had many talents.

I stared into the bowl in front of me. It looked like a watery soup with some pinkish chunks floating in it.

"Walrus blubber," Dr. Deerwin whispered in my ear. "High calories. Zero carbs."

My belly was still a little queasy from the plane ride and the snowmobile trek, but I was also really hungry. How do you eat blubber, anyway? Spoon? Fork? Tongs? None of the above. Panuk and Uki reached into their bowls and pulled out big chunks with their fingers.

I looked at Penelope. She shrugged. And then she reached right in. I followed her lead. I plucked out what looked like a nice juicy piece and popped it into my mouth. It did not taste like chicken. It did not taste like anything I'd ever tasted before. A little rubbery. A little oily. But not terrible. I'd had way worse in the school cafeteria. And at least it erased the taste of Onion Chippies.

While I chewed (and chewed and chewed), I looked around the trailer. The walls were covered with maps and weather charts, like you'd expect in a research center, but one thing stood out. It was a wanted poster. And the guy whose face was on it looked like a real desperado. Stringy hair. Beady eyes. Missing teeth. Scar on his chin. He made Voldemort look like a choirboy.

WANTED
←—Dead or Alive—→
(Dead would be better.)

Armed and Dangerous.
Really Bad Breath.
$10,000 Reward

"Who's *that*?" I asked.

"That's Vin Broacher," said Panuk as he wolfed down another chunk of *aivik*.

"Aka Broacher the Poacher," said Uki. There was a little shiver in her voice, and not from the cold.

"He's the meanest, most dangerous dude in Alaska," said Panuk. "He shoots, he traps, he steals. No animal is safe while he's around."

Not even polar bears? I wondered.

"If you ever see him…" said Panuk.

"Run!" said Uki.

They didn't have to tell me twice. Just

looking at Broacher's face was enough to give me nightmares. Speaking of which—by the time we finished eating, it was just about time for bed. We'd been traveling for about twelve hours straight and I was wiped out. I could see that Penelope was exhausted, too. But I didn't see any beds anywhere.

"Where do you guys sleep?" I asked.

"Look up!" said Uki. She stood on her tiptoes and started pulling down little one-person bunks from the sides of the trailer. When she was finished, there wasn't any room to move. So we all pulled off our kamaak, stashed our sweaters and parkas, and turned in for the night. I was in one of the bottom bunks, with Dr. Deerwin right above me. It was like being nestled in my own cozy cocoon. I preferred to think of it as a sleep pod.

Panuk was the last one into his bunk. He reached out and clicked off the ceiling light. And just like that, it was totally dark, inside and out. I couldn't see my fingers in front of my face. But I knew they were there. I could still smell the blubber.

Then, from the other side of the trailer, I heard Uki singing. Not in English.

Not in any language I'd ever heard. It sounded sweet, like a lullaby.

"Wee-hee-ahh, Wee-hee ya hah…"

Uki had a really pretty voice. I wanted to hear more. I wanted to ask for an English translation. But as soon as I closed my eyes, I zzzzzzzzzzzzz…

CHAPTER 13

NIBBLES IN THE NIGHT

A few hours later, my eyes popped open. I realized that I had a big problem: I really had to pee! I'd held it all day long, but now my internal organs were screaming out to take care of it. Or else.

I tried to move really slowly and softly so I wouldn't wake anybody else up. I wriggled out of my sleep pod and put my feet on the floor. Even through my thermal socks, it was freezing cold. The thought of walking to the outhouse in the dark was a little scary, but not as scary as wetting my bed. (Been there, done that, don't want to talk about it.) I tiptoed across the floor to where I left my kamaak. Suddenly, I felt something run across my toes.

I jumped! I screamed! I bumped my head on the top of Panuk's bunk! He woke up and flicked on his flashlight, and aimed it at the floor. I saw a bunch of brown fur balls scurry across the trailer and disappear through little cracks in the walls.

I screamed again. Not proud of it. Now everybody else was awake.

"W-W-What's happening?" asked Penelope.

I jumped onto a chair and pointed at the floor. But there was nothing there. The fur balls had totally disappeared.

"Don't worry," said Panuk. "They're just lemmings, looking for midnight snacks. They won't bite."

I looked down by the door, where I'd left my knapsack. There was a big hole chewed right

through the middle compartment, and there were holiday sprinkles and bits of red and green frosting everywhere.

So much for Grandma Dotty's Christmas cookies.

CHAPTER 14

A TRIPPY TREK

Beep! Beep!
The next morning, we were up at the crack of dawn (which looked pretty much like the crack of noon around there). We had power bars and OJ for breakfast and then headed out across the tundra. Dr. Deerwin was holding the tracking antenna up in the air, trying to get a stronger signal. Penelope and I followed right behind her.
Clomp. Clomp.
It was my first time on snowshoes and it was not going great. It felt like trying to walk with tennis rackets strapped to my feet. I knew snowshoes were supposed to add extra traction on the snow, but for me they were just another way to embarrass myself. Penelope was doing way

better than I was. And naturally, Dr. Deerwin was strolling along like she was wearing beach sandals. When it came to the great outdoors, she was great at everything.

Suddenly Dr. Deerwin stopped. She looked down at the tracking device. She moved the antenna around slowly—up and down, side to side.

Beep! BEEP! Beep! BEEP!

"PB2 is nearby!" she said. "Keep your eyes peeled."

I turned around slowly in a complete circle. The last thing I needed was to be ambushed by a polar bear. I could already picture Mom saying "I told you so!" at my funeral. But I didn't see anything. We started walking again. Clomp. Clomp.

Then I heard Penelope shout.

"L-L-Look!" She was pointing to the horizon. I squinted. Sure enough. Something out there was moving!

Penelope started running toward whatever it was as fast as she could. (On snowshoes, that's not very fast.) Dr. Deerwin dropped her antenna and yelled at Penelope to come back, but she wasn't paying any attention. So Dr. Deerwin started running after her. I followed in their tracks, doing my best to keep up.

I didn't see the little ridge in the snow until it was too late. I tripped over my snowshoes and did a total face-plant. When I lifted my head up, I could hear Penelope shouting.

"It's a t-tern!" she said.

A *what*?

CHAPTER 15

THE LEFTOVER

I pulled myself up and trudged over to where Penelope was kneeling in the snow. She was holding something small and fluffy in her hand.

Turns out a tern is a bird. And this one was an *arctic* tern—which, according to Penelope, was something pretty special. Problem was, he wasn't supposed to be here this time of year.

"He sh-sh-should have migrated s-south by now," said Penelope.

Leave it to my friend Penelope Deerwin to find the last migratory bird in Alaska. If you know anything about Penelope, you know that she's kind of a bird whisperer. Of all the critters in the world, she loves birds best. She even has her own pet owl named Lila, who she rescued as an owlet and raised all by herself. And she has a really special way of talking to animals, birds especially.

"Don't worry, baby, we're here to help you."

Did you notice that? I almost forgot. When she talks to birds or animals, Penelope doesn't stutter at all. She can't explain it. Neither can I. It's just one more thing that makes her like no other person I've ever met.

Dr. Deerwin pulled off her gloves and ran her hands over the tern's whole body, from beak to tail feathers. The bird pecked a little at Dr. Deerwin's hand, but didn't try to get away. No wonder. Poor little guy was half-frozen. He was really lucky that an arctic fox hadn't already gobbled him up.

"Fractured ulna," said Dr. Deerwin. (That's "broken wing" for us civilians.) "That's why he got stuck here when all his friends took off."

Penelope held the tern right up to her face. He gave a little peep, like he somehow knew he was totally safe. And he was.

"We'll fix you up, baby," Penelope said. "I promise."

Penelope tucked the tern under her parka. And that put an end to the polar bear search for the day. Dr. Deerwin walked back to pick up the antenna and turned off the locator device. She led the way as we followed our snowshoe tracks back to the research center. I concentrated on not falling on my face.

When we opened the door to the trailer, Panuk and Uki were inside checking weather reports and tinkering with the transmitter.

"L-L-Look what we found!" said Penelope. She was very excited.

She opened the flap of her parka and pulled out the rescued tern.

Now Panuk and Uki were excited, too. They rubbed their hands together.

"Yum!" said Panuk. "Dinner!"

Penelope pulled the bird back under her parka and shook her head so hard that her braids flipped across her face.

"N-No!" said Penelope. "*N-Not* dinner!"

Penelope sat everybody down and explained why arctic terns are unique. How they fly all the way from Alaska to Antarctica and back again every year.

"L-Longest m-migration of any animal *ever*!" she said.

I could tell that Panuk and Uki were impressed by Penelope's grasp of bird trivia. She knew a lot of stuff about arctic creatures that they didn't know, even though they'd lived in Alaska all their lives. Maybe they just specialized in polar bears.

Dr. Deerwin found her medical bag and pulled out a roll of something labeled MICROPORE TAPE. She cut off a strip and used it to wrap the tern's side.

"We need to immobilize the wing so it can heal on its own," she said.

"Hear that, baby?" Penelope said to the tern. "You're going to be good as new in no time!"

I saw Panuk cock his head. He looked puzzled. I knew what he was thinking.

"Hey," he said to Penelope, "how come you're not..."

"S-S-Stuttering?" said Penelope. "Th-That's only when I talk to p-people!"

Panuk looked a little confused. I couldn't blame him. Took me a while to adjust to it, too. Penelope is a very complex person.

Once Panuk and Uki realized that the tern was not on the menu, they helped us put together a little nest with a washcloth and some cotton balls. Uki put her face low to the table where the bird was resting.

"Can I pet him?" she asked.

"G-Gently," said Penelope. "L-Like this." She stroked her finger lightly over the tern's head and down the back of his neck. Uki followed her example.

"So soft!" she said.

"Well, if he's going to be part of the family," said Panuk, "he needs a name."

Uki wrinkled her brow, thinking hard. Then her eyes lit up.

"Nukilik!" she said. She looked at Penelope. "It means 'strong one.'"

"P-Perfect," said Penelope. Then she looked the bird in the eye. "I'll just call you Nuki for short."

After that, we got an eyedropper and fed Nuki his first good meal in a long time. Warm milk mixed with secret ingredients from the bottom of my backpack—leftover crumbs and Christmas sprinkles.

I believe Grandma Dotty's cookies have healing powers.

CHAPTER 16

GARBAGE IN, GARBAGE OUT

Two polar nights later…

I was really frustrated. And really worried. We'd been in Alaska four whole days and we hadn't seen a single polar bear. Not even a paw print. I was starting to think this whole polar bear operation was kind of hopeless. But tonight everything was going to change. Panuk promised.

We were all crammed into the research center's Jeep. Dr. Deerwin and Panuk were in front. I was wedged into the backseat with Penelope and Uki. You'd think that Dr. Deerwin would be driving, since she was the only adult, but you'd be wrong. Panuk was behind the wheel. Uki said he'd been driving since he was ten. Up here in the wilderness, she said, "No license, no problem."

We'd been traveling for about twenty minutes, which felt like forever. At night, the tundra looked even emptier. And darker. And scarier. I was just praying we wouldn't run out of gas. After a while, I could see a little yellow glow in the distance. I got very excited.

"Is that the Northern Lights??" I asked. I got my phone ready to snap a picture for Grandma Dotty.

"Nope," said Uki, "just the light from town."

"T-Town?" said Penelope. "W-Why are we heading t-toward t-town?"

Panuk turned off the bare tundra onto something that looked like an actual road. A sign said, NIKSIK—10 MILES.

"You'll see," he said.

Ten miles later, Panuk was driving slowly around a huge snowbank. It looked like it had been pushed together by a bulldozer. It was dirty and gray and about three times taller than the Jeep. As we came around the other side, I started to smell something really gross. Dr. Deerwin held the antenna out the window. I held my nose. I looked around. We were smack in the middle of a giant landfill. Which is a polite name for a garbage dump. All around us were piles of junk and heaps of trash—half-eaten turkeys, moldy bread, rotten vegetables. You name it. If it stunk, it was there.

This was *not* what I signed up for. If I wanted to smell garbage, I'd just go dumpster diving back in Hills Village. What did this have to do with polar bear research?

"What the heck are we doing here?" I asked.

BEEP! BEEP!

"Shhhhh!" said Uki. "Just wait!"

Dr. Deerwin had the locator device on her lap. She leaned out the window and held the antenna up higher. Panuk drove forward very slowly, a few feet at a time. Then he stopped. He switched from low beams to high beams.

"Look!" he said.

And, suddenly, there it was! Caught in the headlights. An actual polar bear!

My heart started pounding like crazy. Penelope practically climbed over my shoulders to get a better look. The bear stared right at us.

What took you so long?

"Fantastic," said Dr. Deerwin.

"He's b-b-beautiful!" whispered Penelope.

She was right. It was a magnificent animal.

Probably five feet tall at the shoulder and twelve feet from snout to tail. There was a scraggly-looking tracking collar around his neck.

"That's PB1!" said Panuk proudly. "I told you!"

PB1 didn't seem bothered by the lights. He went right back to his business, which was scrounging for food. He picked up a Domino's pizza box in his jaws and shook it. When a couple of stale crusts fell out, he chomped them down. Then he nosed his way into a greasy Burger King bag and came out with a mouthful of fries.

I stopped being excited, and starting getting sad. Then mad. This was pathetic! PB1 should be out on the ice, breathing the sea air, lying in wait for unsuspecting seals. Not munching on leftovers in a trash pile!

"What now?" I asked.

Panuk turned to Uki.

"Get the gun," he said.

CHAPTER 17

BEAR'S-EYE!

He meant the *dart* gun. The kind that shoots animal tranquilizers, not bullets. Whew!

Uki reached behind the seat and grabbed it, all black and sleek-looking. She handed it to Panuk, very carefully. Dr. Deerwin put the antenna and tracking device down on the floor. She took the gun from Panuk and loaded in a huge syringe—twice as big as the one for my flu shot. Then she opened her door slowly and whispered, "Don't move!"

The rest of us sat frozen inside the Jeep like we were watching the world's most exciting drive-in movie.

Dr. Deerwin slipped out around the front of the Jeep. So stealthy! She raised the gun up to her shoulder. I heard a little pop. The dart hit the polar bear right in the behind!

He twisted his head around like he wanted to pull it out with his teeth, but he couldn't reach it. He started to stumble around the trash heap, knocking up against a rusty refrigerator and tripping over an old car battery. He looked like me on snowshoes. Before long, he just kind of gave up and collapsed in a furry heap. PB1 was down!

Dr. Deerwin walked over and gave the bear a few gentle pokes in the side. Then she waved for us all to come out of the Jeep. Panuk, Uki, and

Penelope raced over for a look. I took my sweet time, just in case the bear was faking it—in which case I'd probably be the lone survivor. By the time I walked up, Dr. Deerwin was already working on the bear with a bunch of stuff she'd pulled out of her pockets. She was taking blood samples, injecting vitamins, adjusting the fit on the transmitter collar, and writing all the data down in her waterproof notebook.

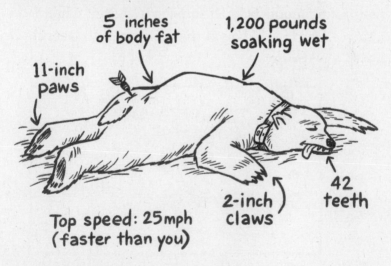

5 inches of body fat

1,200 pounds soaking wet

11-inch paws

2-inch claws

42 teeth

Top speed: 25mph (faster than you)

"*Ursus maritimus*," she said. "'Bear of the sea.' Magnificent, right?"

"S-So p-powerful," said Penelope.

"So awesome," said Panuk.

"So *huge*," said Uki.

I agreed with Uki. Even lying down, PB1 looked bigger than the Jeep. His massive belly was moving in and out and clouds of steam were puffing from his mouth. His breath smelled like fish and french fries.

I pulled out my phone and snapped a photo of the whole crazy scene. I had to share this once-in-a-lifetime moment with somebody! Later, when I had cell service, I'd send the picture off to Georgia with a warning:

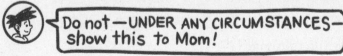

Do not—UNDER ANY CIRCUMSTANCES—show this to Mom!

My mother is pretty level-headed, but I knew she would freak out if she realized that her firstborn child was this close to an apex predator, even if he was knocked out cold.

After Dr. Deerwin finished her checkup, she pulled another big syringe out of her pocket. The wake-up drug.

"Everybody back to the Jeep," she said. Penelope gave the bear one last pat on the paw, then we all moved away. Dr. Deerwin jabbed the needle into PB1's thigh and then hustled us all along. We crammed into the Jeep, rolled up the windows, locked the doors, and waited.

After a few minutes, PB1 lifted his head, then kind of rolled himself over, like a chubby dad trying to get out of a La-Z-Boy recliner. He looked a little unsteady at first. Then he stumbled off between the garbage piles—gone like a ghost. As Panuk started to back the Jeep out, I thought I saw something else moving around in the dark. A human! A sanitation worker? A lost hiker? Or maybe...Broacher the

Poacher?? Nah. Probably just my overactive imagination.

On our way out of the dump, we squished through piles of rotten eggs, disposable diapers, and leftover bait.

"Let's eat!" said Panuk.

CHAPTER 18

SOMETHING FISHY ABOUT THIS BUNCH

When Panuk drove out of the other side of the landfill, we were in the middle of Niksik. This place gave "small town" a whole new meaning. It didn't even have a stoplight. Just a stop sign. Which Panuk totally ignored. So what? There was nobody else on the road. And the police cars were probably frozen anyway.

We passed a general store, which was also the post office. And a school building, which was also the courthouse. There was a church and a gas station and a couple of bars—the kind where you'd expect to see pirates drinking rum.

There were a few big yellow streetlights and

some white flakes were starting to fall. It was like being inside a giant snow globe.

Panuk turned down a side street lined with tiny houses. He pulled up to the house at the very end. It had an A-frame roof, a metal chimney, and a rickety porch. Out front was a pack of wolves!

"Home sweet home," said Panuk.

Panuk opened his door, but I refused to move. No need to get eaten alive.

Sure enough. As soon as Panuk stepped out of the Jeep, the wolf pack was all over him. RIP, my too-handsome friend.

I looked closer. My bad. They weren't wolves. They were huskies. Easy mistake in the dark. The big furry dogs went crazy over Panuk and Uki. They jumped up and licked their faces like they hadn't seen them in ages. When I got out of the Jeep with Penelope, the huskies jumped all over us, too. In fact, they practically knocked us over.

"Down, guys!" said Penelope. The dogs stopped jumping and took a step back. Amazing. I don't know how she does it.

"Wow," said Panuk. "You sure have a way with animals!"

There was admiration in his voice. And something else. I couldn't put my finger on it. But I didn't like it.

"Th-Thanks," said Penelope. She sounded a little proud and a little embarrassed at the same time. She gave each of the dogs a pat on the head as she walked through the pack.

Panuk led the way up to the porch and opened the front door. Suddenly I saw bright lights from inside and heard loud talking and laughing. And I mean *loud*! When we stepped into the living room, there were Inuit of all ages, shapes, and sizes crammed into every corner. More people per square foot than I'd ever seen. There wasn't even room for people to sit down.

A big man with a wrinkled face walked up to Panuk and Uki and gave them big hugs.

"This is our uncle Tarkik," said Panuk. "He just got back from fishing."

Panuk waved his arms to get the attention of the crowd and then introduced us by shouting and pointing at our heads. "Hey, everybody! This is Rafe! And this is Penelope! And this is the world-famous Dr. Deerwin!"

Then everybody came over and greeted us with a *kunik*. Not a kiss, really. More like a quick cheek-to-cheek rub.

They were all so smiley and friendly, like they'd known us all their lives.

"Is this some kind of a party?" I asked Uki. I practically had to yell into her ear over the noise.

"Not really," she yelled back. "Up here, when you bring back a catch or something from a hunt, you share it with the whole neighborhood. Uncle Tarkik caught a bunch of fish. So he invited everybody over to get their cut!"

I liked that tradition. Very humanitarian. Kind

of like me sharing my extra tater tots with my pals in the cafeteria, only on a larger scale.

It was probably about twenty below zero outside. But inside it was so toasty I was starting to sweat. The whole place was filled with smoke from the fireplace and steam from the stove. *What's cooking?* I wondered. *Please, let it not be more walrus blubber.*

CHAPTER 19

YUKON YUMMM!

What a relief. No blubber in sight. But there was plenty of other stuff. *Delicious* stuff! We had some of Uncle Tarkik's fish, which was arctic cod, seared and salty. Really good! There was some fruit called Baffin berries, kind of like a polar version of raspberries, and warm flatbread, like pizza without the sauce.

I had to stand while I ate, with my plate balanced in one hand. I was wedged between two ladies who were talking about heating oil prices. Dr. Deerwin was in a corner discussing cod migration with Uncle Tarkik and his buddies. Panuk had found a place to sit at the bottom of the stairs, and—big surprise—he found a place for Penelope right next to him. They were practically cheek to cheek. I couldn't hear what they were talking about, but Penelope was sure smiling a lot.

That feeling I didn't like was coming back, but worse. I realized that I definitely liked things better at BushyTail, when it was just me and Penelope. She probably thought I was yesterday's news. I thought about trying to wedge myself between the two of them on the stairs and remind Penelope about all of our shared adventures with the critters at BushyTail. But I wasn't sure I'd be welcome. I felt a little ache inside, and it wasn't heartburn. Compared to an authentic Inuit bear expert, I knew I could never stack up.

I felt somebody tap me on the elbow. I looked down.

"I'm Amka! I'm Panuk and Uki's mom!"

An Inuit lady was standing right in front of me. She was so short that she barely came up to my middle shirt button. When she smiled, she looked like a grown-up version of Uki, except with one gold tooth. She had a leather hair band that pushed her black hair back from her shiny forehead. She piled another helping of cod onto my plate.

"Too skinny," she said, poking my waist. "You need more insulation."

"Thanks," I said. "But I'm really..."

No use. She added a pile of flatbread, too. Then a bunch of Baffin berries. Then she stood up on tiptoes and leaned into my ear.

"Uki says you make her laugh," she said.

I wanted to ask if Uki was laughing *with* me or laughing *at* me. I was pretty sure I knew the answer. But before I could say anything else, I heard the front door open. A man in a thick parka and fur collar walked in. He had an official-looking badge on his sleeve, like some kind of polar ranger. He stamped his feet at the front entrance and looked toward the men who were talking in the corner.

"The *grozny* is back!" the ranger called out.

I could see the other men shake their heads. Uncle Tarkik made the kind of face Principal Stricker makes when she finds out there's another stink bomb in the boys' room.

What the heck is a *grozny*? Some other kind of dangerous arctic critter? A bad Yukon snowstorm? A polar poltergeist?

Whatever it is, nobody liked the sound of it. And it pretty much put a damper on the party. Pretty soon, Panuk and Uki decided it was time to leave.

I would have asked about the *grozny* on the way home, but I fell asleep as soon as I hit the car seat. My face was pressed against the cold window all the way back to the research center, but I didn't even notice. I was so groggy when we got back, I just about fell into my bunk. I saw Penelope feeding Nuki some leftover Baffin berries she'd stashed in her pocket. Such a good caretaker.

I was so stuffed that I thought my bunk might collapse under my weight. I couldn't even lie on my belly. It was as round as a bowling ball. When I rolled over to find a comfortable position, I could see out the tiny window next to my bed—all the way to the Chukchi Sea in the distance. I stared. I squinted. What's that?? Somewhere out on the water, I saw a moving light. Or did I? Impossible. The water was frozen this time of year, right?

I figured it must've been a shooting star. Or an ice mirage. I rolled over again, worrying about Penelope smiling at Panuk and laughing at me and about a *grozny* coming to grab me in my sleep. And then I let out the world's loudest, smelliest codfish belch.

So gross. So inappropriate. So me.

CHAPTER 20

PALACE OF THE PRINCE

Oh, P-P-Panuk! That's t-terrific!"

"Nothing to it!"

The next morning, I woke up to the sound of talking and laughing from outside. It was Penelope and Panuk, having some kind of fun frolic without me.

Serves me right for sleeping late.

I crawled out of bed, hitched up my thermal underpants, and opened the trailer door a crack. There they were, right out front, in plain sight. And I couldn't believe what I was seeing. Panuk was teaching Penelope how to build an igloo! And he was obviously a pro at it. While Penelope watched, he cut out chunks of snow with a big saw and then stacked them into a dome. Perfectly balanced. Perfectly symmetrical. And he wasn't even using a tape measure! Pure Inuit instinct all the way. I guess he was born with it. Then he put his gloves on top of Penelope's gloves and showed her how to rub the edges off the snow blocks for a perfect fit. Pretty smooth, Panuk, pretty smooth.

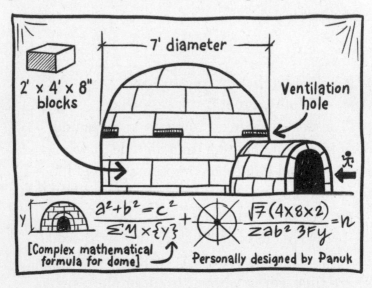

2' × 4' × 8" blocks

7' diameter

Ventilation hole

y

$$\dfrac{a^2+b^2=c^2}{\Sigma y \times \{y\}} + \dfrac{\sqrt{7}\,(4\times8\times2)}{zab^2\ 3Fy} = n$$

[Complex mathematical formula for dome]

Personally designed by Panuk

I felt so left out that I slammed the door shut. Over at the other end of the trailer, Uki and Dr. Deerwin had their noses buried in topographical tundra maps. Nuki the tern peeped his head up from his nest, but I wasn't in any mood to be cheered up by his chirping. I grabbed a container of cereal off the counter and poured myself a heaping bowlful. Then I sat on my bunk and started chomping away. Loudly. I didn't care who heard me.

What was going on here? I wondered. Where had I gone wrong? I made this whole trip to experience the wilderness and get closer to Penelope—and there she was playing house with another man! Well, I thought, two can play at that game. I looked over at Uki. She looked up from her map and looked back at me. Her eyes opened wide.

"Rafe!" she shouted. "You're eating reindeer feed!"

I never spit so fast.

RAFE 0, BEARS 3

When Dr. Deerwin asked me to help her calibrate the antenna that afternoon, I saw my chance at revenge. I made a special point of inviting Uki to come along. Panuk was busy greasing his snowmobile out back and Penelope was napping after her igloo-building efforts. Not that I would have asked her to come anyway. Payback is sweet. Besides, Uki said that her tracking data showed that PB2 should be in the area. Wouldn't it be great if I was the one to find a polar bear in its natural habitat without Panuk or Penelope helping?

Dream on, Rafe, dream on.

We'd been out for about twenty minutes when

the tracking device started beeping. But just in quick snatches. Nothing steady. Uki held up the antenna while Dr. Deerwin tried to home in on the signal.

"*This* way!" she said, pointing north. At least I *think* it was north. Hard to tell around here. Anyway, I was just trying to keep up. I was getting a little more confident on my snowshoes, but Uki and Dr. Deerwin were way ahead of me, almost out of sight on the other side of a snowdrift. I could hardly hear the beeping.

"Hey, guys—wait up!" I shouted.

Uki and Dr. Deerwin were standing close together about twenty yards away. Uki held the antenna up and turned around in a slow circle.

"She should be close!" she called out.

I didn't want to be a cold blanket, but I'd heard that before. I figured the electronics must be wacky. I looked around in every direction. There was nothing for miles. Not a creature was stirring, not even a lemming. This was just another wild goose chase—polar bear edition. My feet were aching. My calves were burning. I put one snowshoe in front of the other. And then...

Poof! I was gone.

The next thing I knew, I landed hard on my rear end. I looked up to see a small patch of sunlight where I'd fallen through the snow. I was in a small dark space underneath. It smelled like a wet gym sock stuffed with fish guts. Somebody was snoring—like Grandma Dotty when she loses her inhaler.

I felt my arms and legs. Nothing broken. I looked around. It was so dark I could hardly see. Whoa! I realized that I almost landed on two little stuffed bears. Crazy! Who would bury two teddy bears out here in the snow?

Hold on...

They weren't teddy bears. They were *real* bears! Cubs. Asleep against a giant pile of fur. A giant *breathing* pile of fur!

One thought flashed through my brain: *PB2! I found you!*

BEEP! BEEP!

I saw a glove punch through the snow from above. I'd know that glove anywhere. I grabbed it. Dr. Deerwin pulled me out like she was landing a carp. Uki was pointing the antenna right at the hole I just came out of. The locator was beeping on overdrive. Dr. Deerwin reached down and clicked off the sound.

"Congratulations, Rafe!" she whispered. "You just located a world-class polar bear den!" We all stepped away from the hole. Then Dr. Deerwin gave us very clear instructions on what to do next.

"Don't scream. Don't run. Just back up slowly and walk away."

If our luck held out, maybe PB2 wouldn't wake up, chase us down, and feed us to her cubs for lunch. Even though it was all pretty scary, I could tell that Uki was really excited. It's not every day that you come across a mama bear and two babies. This was going to give her a real leg up on her next school science report. And guess who she had to thank for it? *Me!*

"We never would have found them without you, Rafe!" said Uki. She leaned over and gave me a little hug, which felt pretty darned good.

"Nothing to it," I said.

We got back to the research center in record time, looking over our shoulders the whole way. Penelope was out front when we walked up. I couldn't wait to tell her about my near-death experience in the bear den. But she hardly noticed me. Didn't even *look* at me.

"Isn't it p-p-perfect?" she asked. She was looking at Panuk's finished igloo.

She'd obviously been busy adding some final touches while I was away, and now she couldn't stop talking about how much fun it was to build and how much she learned from Panuk.

"And look!" she said. "It's so strong that you can stand on the top and not break it. Panuk said so!"

Sure enough, Penelope climbed right up the side of the dome and stood on the tippy-top with her hands on her hips, like a statue.

Chronic overachiever

Chronic underperformer

I tried to look interested, but I wasn't. Not at all. But as I watched Penelope strike a pose on top of her ice house, I began to hatch a plan of my own. A *great* plan. A Khatchadorian classic.

CHAPTER 22

ANYTHING YOU IGLOO,
I CAN DO BETTER

The next morning, I was up before dawn. I
think. Again, hard to tell around here. Before
anybody else was stirring, I chomped down a
couple of power bars to build up my strength and
then headed outside.

Have I mentioned how cold it was in Alaska?
I think I have, but it's worth mentioning again.
Try to remember the coldest you've ever felt. Like
after a freezing shower. Or after walking home
through an ice storm. Or the kind of cold your
throat feels after drinking a Swifty's Slushy too
fast. Compared to Alaska cold, that's *nothing*!
When I walked outside, the air hit me like a brick.

A frozen brick. It was so cold it took my breath away. But I fought through it. I stamped my feet and rubbed my gloves together. I pulled up my snow pants and flipped up my hood. I had work to do.

My plan was simple, but grand. I was about to build an igloo of my own. But not just any igloo— the biggest, classiest, coolest igloo the tundra had ever known. The Taj Mahal of igloos. The Buckingham Palace of igloos. The Stonehenge of igloos. The Hogwarts of igloos! That would take the wind out of Panuk's sails and get Penelope to notice me again.

I had a mission. I had ambition. Did I have any actual skills? Of course not. But that never stopped me before. I picked up Panuk's snow saw and started cutting out big chunks of snow. To think warm thoughts, I pictured workers on the Egyptian pyramids, sweltering under the desert sun. It didn't help. I pictured the Natives on Easter Island raising huge stone heads under the tropical heat. That didn't help, either.

But once I got into my rhythm, wonder of wonders, I started to forget the cold. Mind over matter, they call it. And it actually worked! Slowly, my walls started to rise. Higher and higher. Before long, my ice dome was looking pretty big. Massive, in fact! Twice as big as the dinky igloo Panuk designed. Who's the big thinker *now*?

Once my basic structure was in place, I let my imagination run wild. I added a picture window and a back porch. I carved two pink flamingos for the front yard. Actually, they were *white* flamingos, but you get the idea. I knew the bird theme would appeal to Penelope. And speak of the devil…

I had just finished smoothing the outside of my entire dome when I saw Penelope, Panuk, and Uki all peeking out of the front trailer window. Perfect timing.

"Hey, everybody!" I shouted. "Look!"

Penelope rubbed the frost off the window so she could see better, and I could tell she was impressed. She gave me a smile and a thumbs-up, which made me feel like a million bucks.

Now it was time for my *pièce de résistance*, which is French for the most amazing part of all. I had cleverly built steps up the back of the igloo so that I could reach the top without climbing up the sides. I couldn't wait to stand up there and prove how sturdy my construction was. I waved toward the trailer and then ran up my snow-stairs. I stepped onto the top of the igloo like a conquering hero. I was so high up that I could see the whole top of the trailer. I could almost see all the way to the sea! I could see Penelope and Uki and Panuk moving their lips behind the window, but I could only imagine what they were saying. Great stuff, no doubt.

I folded my arms over my chest the way movie

heroes do after the battle has been won. That's what this was like. That's exactly how I felt.

That's when my roof caved in.

(Rough translation: What a fool!)

CHAPTER 23

FAR AND WIDE

I was still feeling a little embarrassed the next morning. I had a lump on my butt from where I landed on my igloo floor and a bump on my head from where my ice roof collapsed on top of me. When I peeked out the trailer window during breakfast, I could see the pile of toppled snow blocks just sitting there, like they were mocking me. And of course, they wouldn't just melt away. In this miserable climate, they'd be there forever. Perma-shame.

Then, believe it or not, somebody found a way to cheer me up. And you'll never guess who it was.

It was Panuk.

After we finished eating, he asked Dr. Deerwin if we could take a break from bear research for the day and go on a hike—just us kids. Dr. Deerwin was so distracted with all her scientific reports that she actually said yes. Then she thought about it. Then she spent the next twenty minutes making sure that we were totally prepared for our trek. She loaded our pockets with power bars and beef jerky. Since we were in a dead zone for cell phones, she gave us a spare compass. She even handed us a couple of signal flares, just in case. And then she pointed at each of us, one after the other.

"Stick tight," she said. "Nobody leaves anybody else's sight, got it?"

We all nodded. We got it.

"Don't worry," said Panuk, "this is our turf."

"We know the tundra like the back of our hands," added Uki.

I could tell that Dr. Deerwin trusted them. She knew they both had solid wilderness skills. And besides, she had plenty of work do on the research study. She was trying to map out all the possible locations of PB3—the biggest bear of all—who was still nowhere to be found. As we headed out the door, Dr. Deerwin made sure we were all wrapped up, buttoned up, and zipped up. Then she stood at the door watching us hike off.

When I looked back, I could still see her at the door until the trailer was just a speck in the distance. As soon as we were out of sight, Panuk called us all together for a tribal conference. That's when he let us in on his secret. This was no ordinary hike he had planned. It was a big adventure. He was taking us all the way to the Chukchi Sea! The very last place Dr. Deerwin would have wanted us to go.

CHAPTER 24

GO WITH THE FLOE

All I knew about the Chukchi Sea was that it was huge—hundreds of thousands of square miles of open water going all the way from Alaska to Siberia. I'd only seen pictures on the internet and little glimpses from my window, so I couldn't wait to see it in person. Let's face it, once you've seen one stretch of Alaskan tundra, you've pretty much seen it all. But an ocean view? That sounded really exciting. And I could see that Penelope was excited, too.

But it was no pleasure stroll. It took us all morning to get close, with a few power bar and beef jerky breaks along the way. Panuk let me set the pace, and I was slowly getting more confident in my snowshoes. I kept my head low and concentrated on staying vertical.

Suddenly I heard Panuk shout, "Water, ho!"

I looked up and there it was! Instead of endless snow, we were looking out at an endless sea. The Chukchi was so big it seemed to go on forever. I expected to see a solid sheet of ice, but it was more like a puzzle of floating chunks mixed with churning slush. And there were icebergs! As tall as my house back home.

"This is *a-m-mazing*!" said Penelope. With each syllable, her breath came out in cute little puffs.

Panuk led us right to the edge, where the tundra dropped off. It was like being on another planet. Scary and weird and beautiful all at the same time.

"How come it's not all frozen solid?" I asked.

"It used to be this time of year," said Uki, "but not anymore. Now it doesn't freeze over until after January. Uncle Tarkik's afraid that pretty soon, it won't freeze at all."

"When that happens," said Panuk, "the bears won't have anywhere to hunt."

"Which m-means they'll s-s-starve!" said Penelope.

Maybe that's what already happened to PB3, I thought. Maybe that's why we can't find him. But I shook that depressing thought out of my head. Enough doom and gloom! This whole situation might have been caused by global warming, but it also looked like the world's most fantastic playground. Like a polar water park. And we were the only customers!

Panuk pulled off his snowshoes and led the way out onto the ice with just his kamaak. He jumped across a break in the water until he was standing on a free-floating chunk of sea ice. Uki followed right behind him and landed on a chunk of her own. Penelope went next, then me. I stepped very carefully. Didn't want to get dunked. I'd already fallen through enough frozen holes for a lifetime. When we looked back, the shoreline was moving away. Or I guess it was the other way around. Anyway, we were explorers in our own ice world. The air was so fresh that it didn't matter how cold it was. My heart was beating so fast it was keeping me warm.

Panuk was really sure-footed. No shock there. But Uki was just as good. They both knew exactly where to jump, when to shift their weight, how to balance just right. I could tell they'd been doing this all their lives. But I could see that Penelope was determined to keep up. And so was I.

After a few more hops, we all ended up on the same ice floe, about the size of a living room rug. A huge iceberg was floating about twenty yards away. It looked like a partly melted castle. Suddenly we heard a gurgle and a splash behind us. The ice floe started rocking! I looked down and saw a huge shape coming toward us under the water. It was the size of a truck.

"Watch out!" shouted Panuk. "It's a whale!"

Uki grabbed Panuk's arm. Penelope grabbed mine. We looked at each other. Could this really be happening?? Were we about to be whale food?

Arctic Whale

Me Junior Tadpole

The whale slid right underneath our ice floe. We could feel it bumping us from underneath. Then it came to the surface on the other side. The whale's head was whitish-gray, all shiny and smooth. From where I was standing, we could see one tiny black eye. And I swear it was looking right at me!

"He's about to blow!" said Uki. She turned her face away and covered her nose. A second later, I knew why.

I saw the hole on the top of the whale's head open up and then a spray shot up about fifteen feet into the air. It turned into a cloudy mist and then it fell right on top of us. It smelled really bad—like getting a fish shower. Then the whale opened its mouth. That was even *worse*!

Whale-Breath Odor Components:

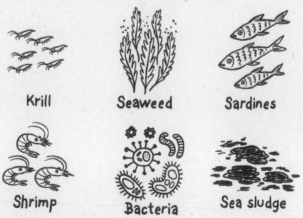

Krill   Seaweed   Sardines

Shrimp   Bacteria   Sea sludge

As soon as the whale was done blowing, it lowered its head and disappeared under the ice chunks. All we could see were the little swirls and ripples it left behind.

Then, from the other side of the iceberg, we heard men yelling. Loud and angry. I'm no language expert, but to me, it sounded like Russian.

CHAPTER 25

THROWING AWAY THEIR SHOT

As we looked back toward the iceberg, the prow of a huge ship came out from behind it. The ship was creaky and rusty and the front edge had big teeth for cutting through ice. There was black smoke burping out of a tipsy smokestack, like the exhaust pipe on Grandma Dotty's Volvo. It looked like the kind of boat a supervillain would use for sailing the underworld. We all crouched down on the ice—not that there was any place to hide. We just tried to scrunch together and make ourselves as tiny as possible.

The ship came closer. On the top deck sat an evil-looking machine with a long black tube. It looked like a troll-blaster from Wormhole Advanced Weapons Level.

"What's that big pointy thing?" I asked Panuk.

"Harpoon gun," he said.

"They're whale hunters!" said Uki. Her voice sounded a little sad and a little mad.

As the rest of the ship came into view, we could see crew members in black uniforms running around the deck like ants. They were pointing toward the water where the whale just disappeared. It looked like they were trying to figure out which way it was headed. By now, just about the whole ship had passed by us. I looked up at the stern (that's the back end). Painted in big letters below the railing was the ship's name:

GROZNY

So this is what the polar ranger was warning everybody about!

All of a sudden, we saw a big spout in the distance. The whale was coming up for air again. The spout got the *Grozny* crew even more excited. They knocked into one another as they cranked a big wheel on the side of the harpoon gun. Slowly the gun turned to point in the direction of the whale.

Somebody on deck shouted, *"Pozhar na vole!"*

From where I was, it sounded like "Shoot the harpoon!"

There was a sound like a cannon firing and a big blast of smoke came out of the business end of the black tube. The harpoon shot out with a long piece of yellow rope attached, like the world's thickest fishing line. Penelope buried her face in her hands.

"I c-c-can't l-look," she said.

Just then the whale took a dive. Maybe he saw what was coming. The harpoon flew through the air and made a big splash in the water right behind his tail fluke.

"*Chert voz' mi!*" the harpoon guy shouted.

I could tell from the sound of the words that he missed. Sure enough, the other crew members started whacking him over the head with their sailor caps and kicking the side of the harpoon gun. They were furious!

"The whale's okay!" said Panuk. "He got away!"

Uki and Penelope gave each other a little celebration hug. I gave Panuk a high five. Then I saw the captain come down the ladder from his wheelhouse and start stamping his feet on the deck, pointing at the harpoon gun and then toward the water, back and forth, yelling the whole time. No sense in trying to figure out what he said. But he was really angry. Just imagine your soccer coach after you've kicked the ball into the wrong net. Again. *That* kind of angry.

His face was all red and splotchy and when he

waved his arms, he almost knocked his captain's
cap right off his head.

"Let's get out of here!" said Panuk.

We started to crawl on our hands and knees
across the ice floe, hoping the crew wouldn't spot
us. Panuk got to his feet and jumped onto the next
chunk of ice, heading back toward shore. Uki was
right behind him. Penelope went next. I turned
to take one last look at the *Grozny* before I made
my leap. That was a big mistake. I lost my focus.
My left foot slid off the edge of the ice and went
right into the slushy water with a big splash. I felt
the cold shoot right through to my toenails, and I
screamed in shock at the top of lungs. I heard the

captain shouting. He was looking in our direction.

We'd been spotted!

Panuk was two ice floes ahead of me. He turned around.

"Run, Rafe, run!" he shouted.

CHAPTER 26

THE BIG DIG

Lucky for us, the *Grozny* wasn't exactly built for speed. By the time the captain started turning the prow with the big teeth toward us, we were already climbing back onto shore. I never thought I'd be so happy to touch the cold hard tundra again. Penelope turned around to stick her tongue out at the ship.

"G-G-Go home!" she shouted.

"I thought whaling was banned around here!" I said.

"It is," said Panuk. "But this one ship keeps coming back year after year. Pretty soon, the whales will all be gone."

"Stupid rogue Russkies," said Uki. "They're the *worst*!"

We picked up our snowshoes on the shore. I dumped the slush out of my kamik. Then we headed back toward the research center. We'd spent so much time ice-hopping that it was getting dark. Darker than usual. *Scary* dark. Then it started to snow. Penelope tipped her face up and caught the first flake on her tongue.

"*Qanuk,*" said Panuk.

"*Q-Q-Qanuk!*" Penelope repeated after him.

Great. Now I knew the Inuit word for snowflake. But that was just the beginning. Because there were at least *fifty* different Inuit words for snow. Of course, Panuk knew them all— and he wasn't about to rest until he taught us every single one.

As we trekked along, he pointed out *kanevvluk* (fine snow), *qanikcaq* (snow on the ground), *qengaruk* (snowbank), and on and on. Penelope seemed to be enjoying the vocab lesson, but I was getting a little nervous, especially since we were now up to our knees in *muruaneq* (really deep snow).

It was getting darker. The snow was blowing harder. And the research center was nowhere in sight. We thought we were retracing our steps, but now we weren't so sure.

"Who's got the compass?" asked Panuk. I remembered that we'd divvied up the gear that morning. I had the compass.

"Right here!" I said. I patted my pocket.

Uh-oh.

The compass must have fallen out when I slipped on the ice floe! Thanks to me, our way home was lying somewhere at the bottom of the Chukchi Sea. Nice one, Rafe.

Normally, Panuk and Uki could have navigated by the stars. Problem was, the clouds blocked the stars out. Now the snow was blowing almost sideways. Little ice crystals started stinging my face like a thousand frozen needles. Then the wind started to howl. We all looked around. Nothing but white.

"It's a b-b-blizzard!" shouted Penelope.

"It's a *pirta*!" Panuk shouted back. Now he was starting to get on my nerves. I was hungry. I was exhausted. And I was a little scared, even though I wasn't about to show it, especially in front of Penelope. But secretly, I was starting to wonder if we'd ever find our way back.

We tried to walk a little farther, but it was no use. The wind was so strong it felt like we were pushing against an invisible hand. Panuk looked at Uki. They stopped, then dropped to their knees. What was happening? Were they praying? Were things that bad??

Then they both started digging into the snow, using their gloves like shovels. Slowly but surely, they dug us a little snow cave. It was probably right out of the Inuit Survival Guide. I had to admit I was impressed. I wasn't looking forward to ending up as a snow log.

The snow cave was tiny, but that was the whole idea. When the four of us crammed inside, our body heat started to warm us up. I noticed that Panuk was nestled right up next to Penelope. If I wasn't so pale and frosty, I would have been green with envy.

Outside the cave, the snow was coming down harder, like a thick white curtain. Suddenly, a huge shape appeared outside. I sat up. I blinked. The shape was blurry—just a dim outline in the falling snow.

It was the outline of a *bear*!

Everybody else saw it, too. We all backed up as far as we could into the snow cave, but that still left our kamaak sticking out. Penelope reached into her parka and pulled out a flare. She lit the end and a bright-red flame shot out. She closed her eyes and threw the flare outside the snow cave. We heard a loud roar. Good-bye, cruel world! We were about to be polar bear snacks for sure.

The roar got louder. It was a snowmobile! Dr. Deerwin to the rescue! The snowmobile kicked up a big spray of snow as it pulled up right outside our snow cave. Dr. Deerwin hopped off and leaned in to grab us. She was not happy.

"I thought I told you kids to be careful!" she said. I'd never seen such a stern look on her face.

Panuk and Uki looked embarrassed. I knew they hated to disappoint Dr. Deerwin. She was their hero. Mine, too.

"Penelope!" said Dr. Deerwin. "You should know better!"

"S-Sorry, M-Mom," said Penelope.

I couldn't hold back any longer. We were missing the whole point here.

"Dr. Deerwin, we *saw* him!" I shouted.

"Saw who?" asked Dr. Deerwin.

"PB3!" I pointed to the ground outside the snow

cave. "He was standing right there!" I looked for paw prints, but there weren't any. The snow was falling really hard. Maybe it already covered up the tracks. Or maybe the whole thing was just a mass hallucination. I could tell Dr. Deerwin was in no mood for tall tales.

"All of you!" she said. "In the back!"

She had the cargo sled tied to the rear of the snowmobile. It was like a giant rubber tub on skis. Not the most comfortable ride home, but maybe the bumps were part of our punishment. Dr. Deerwin didn't even look back at us once the whole way.

Under the circumstances, we decided not to tell her about almost being harpooned by Russians.

CHAPTER 27

GLUM CHUMS

Wh-what's wrong, Rafe?"

It was the next morning. I was sitting on a broken snow block at the bottom of my crumbled igloo. I don't know how Penelope knew something was bothering me, but she always picks up on feelings, from animals *and* people.

Thrilled

Peppy

Sad

Morose

Ecstatic

Despondent

Of course, I couldn't tell her one reason that I was upset. I couldn't say that I wished Panuk didn't look like a rock star and possess awesome survival skills and igloo-building talents. I could never in a million years say that I wished she wouldn't pay so much attention to him. So I decided to tell her the *other* thing that was troubling me. Because that was pretty big, too.

"I think I might be just the teeny-weeniest bit homesick," I said.

Penelope dragged over a snow block of her own and sat down right next to me.

"I kn-know what you m-mean," she said.

"Wanna know what I really miss?" I asked.

"S-S-Sure," she said.

I painted the picture for her. This was the time of year when me and Georgia would be running around the Hills Village Mall deciding which earrings to buy for Mom and which scented candle to get for Grandma Dotty. We always bickered, but in the end, we always agreed.

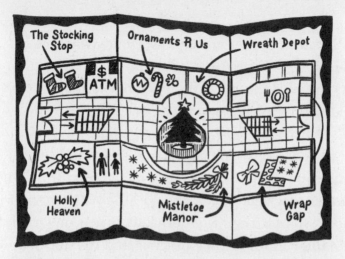

The Stocking Stop · Ornaments Я Us · Wreath Depot

ATM

Holly Heaven · Mistletoe Manor · Wrap Gap

Back at the house, the Christmas tree would already be up in the living room and Mom would have the Celine Dion Christmas album on full repeat.

Penelope nodded. She was a great listener. I kept going.

"Now we're stuck in a place that actually *looks* like the North Pole," I said, "but there's no Christmas spirit at all."

It was at that very second that we heard the sound. Jingle bells. They were coming from a distance, far across the tundra. As usual, the polar twilight made it hard to see, but I thought I could make out a shape coming toward us. Was that a sleigh?? It looked red! And there was a guy with a long beard driving. Could it be? We both stood up. The sleigh came closer. A voice called out.

"Which way to Koyuk?"

Shocker. It wasn't Santa and eight tiny reindeer. It was the two burly dudes from the plane on their dogsled. The dogs had little bells on their collars in case they wandered off. It was one week into their Iditarod race practice and the dudes and dogs were totally lost.

"Koyuk?" Penelope thought for a second, then pointed over her shoulder. "Th-That way!"

I remembered from the map that Koyuk was north of Shaktoolik. Which meant these poor guys were about four hundred miles off course. We didn't have the heart to tell them. We just let them mush away.

As soon as they disappeared, Penelope plunked back down on her snow block. I could tell that she was a little blue, too.

"You kn-kn-know, R-Rafe," she said, "I haven't b-been home for Ch-Christmas in years."

"Really?" I said. "How come?"

As soon as she explained it, I totally understood. She was always away on some animal expedition with her mom, even during the holidays. She'd spent Christmas in Bali, Christmas in Brazil, Christmas in Bangladesh. You name it. Everywhere but home.

"That's crazy," I said.

"D-Don't g-get me wrong," said Penelope, "I l-love my m-mom. I l-love animals. I l-love to t-travel. B-But..."

She didn't even have to finish the sentence. I knew what she meant.

Christmas was all about being at home with

your family in front of a cozy fire with stockings hanging from the mantel. That's exactly what I was longing for, too.

But what could I do about it?

Absolutely nothing.

CHAPTER 28

THESE ARE MY PEOPLE

Did you ever wake up with a one-in-a-million, life-changing idea? Happens to me all the time. In fact, it happened the very next morning. I sat up so fast I almost fell right out of my sleep pod. It was a foolproof plan. Fully hatched. And here's how it went:

If Penelope and I couldn't be home for the holidays, I would bring the holidays to *us*! That's right. I was about to make Christmas on the tundra the very best Christmas ever! I was so excited that I skipped the most important meal of the day. No time. I had more important things to do.

When I stepped outside the trailer, I looked around at my crumbled igloo cubes and smiled.

Because now I had a way to use them. I was about to make lemonade from the lemons life handed me. Seize victory from the jaws of defeat. Turn my frown upside down.

Step One: I shaved the edges off the snow cubes to make them balls instead of rectangles. Step Two: I shaped the balls into different sizes—small, medium, and large. Step Three: I rolled the balls around on the snow to make sure they were sturdy and perfectly round.

As I worked, I noticed Penelope watching me from the window. But I didn't wave to her. I pretended I didn't even see her. I didn't want her to think I was showing off. I wanted her to see how dedicated I was. An artist at work!

If you know anything about me, you probably know that deep down, I have a very creative soul, which I inherited from my mom. She's a great painter. I still remember the first time she told me that I had a good eye.

"What's wrong with the other one?" I asked.

But once she explained it, I felt pretty good. She meant that I can see things that other people don't. And it's true. I can take two ideas that have nothing to do with each other and mash them together to make something new. Like taking a wrecked igloo and turning it into the world's coolest family of snowmen! And women. What could be more Christmas-y than *that*? (I told you it was a genius idea.)

Of course, I had to suffer for my art. Since I had the upper-body strength of a strand of spaghetti, it was really hard to stack the snowman body parts. But I got it done. Before long, I had a whole *family* of snowpeople. Mom, Dad, and two really cute kids.

Now I had to bring them to life. I didn't have any coal to make the eyes. There weren't even any stones or pebbles around. But I noticed that my parka had some spare buttons sewn into the lining.

I plucked them out and—*voilà!*—instant eyeballs.
They looked great, except I was one button short.
So the last snowman looked kind of like a one-eyed
pirate.

Just then, Panuk and Uki rode up on their
snowmobile with a load of groceries. I was really
proud to show off my snow clan.

"Way better than your igloo!" said Panuk.

I think that's what they call faint praise, but I
didn't care, because Uki really seemed to admire
my work. She walked around the snow family,
nodding the whole time.

"Very artistic, Rafe!" she said.

She stared at the one-eyed snowman, then reached into her parka and popped out a spare button. And just like that, my snow guy had a full set of peepers. Perfect!

As Uki headed into the trailer with the groceries, she started singing. But this time, it wasn't one of her Inuit tunes. It was "Jingle Bell Rock." And she could really belt it out.

I was feeling better about Christmas already.

CHAPTER 29

FAST START, HARD STOP

When I walked back into the trailer, Penelope and Uki had their heads together, pointing out the window and chatting about my snow family. Penelope was laughing and smiling, and that made me really happy. My plan was working. But not on everybody.

Dr. Deerwin hadn't even noticed my efforts. She was too busy recalibrating the tracking equipment. And I could tell she was worried. PB3 was still off the grid. Not a beep. Not a blip. And Dr. Deerwin still wasn't convinced that our sighting was the real deal. I moseyed over to the equipment table.

"Maybe PB3 pulled off his tracking collar," I said.

"Possible," said Dr. Deerwin, not even looking up.

"Or maybe he wandered down to Canada," I said.

"Mm-hmm," said Dr. Deerwin. I could tell she didn't buy that theory.

I didn't even want to *think* about the other possibilities—like PB3 was a rug in some rich guy's ski chalet. I got a little shiver, and then I felt Broacher the Poacher's beady eyes staring at me from the wanted poster on the wall. But I shook it off. I had to put all those dark thoughts out of my mind to concentrate on the next phase of my Tundra Christmas:

Finding the perfect Christmas tree!

Foliage was pretty sparse around the research center, but I thought I remembered seeing a few hearty evergreens on our trip from the landing zone. I grabbed my axe and started walking down the trail.

I'd only gone a few yards when Uki caught up to me.

"If you're going a long way," she said, "why don't you take the snowmobile?"

Awkward moment. I was embarrassed to tell Uki that I had no idea how to drive a snowmobile. The truth was, I could barely manage a snowblower.

"I…uh…" I said.

Uki nodded. She got it instantly. "It's easy," she said. "I'll teach you!"

She tugged my sleeve and led me over to Panuk's snowmobile. It was all tricked out with the latest gadgets, but Uki stuck to the basics: Ignition. Throttle. Headlight. Handlebars.

She made it sound so simple. What could go wrong?

I hopped onto the seat. Deluxe padding. Sweet. I slipped on the helmet. Perfect fit. I turned the key and pressed the throttle lever with my thumb. The snowmobile roared and took off like a bull at a rodeo. I grabbed the handlebars and hung on for dear life. When I looked up, I was heading straight for the research center. The engine was so loud I could barely hear Uki yelling.

"Turn, Rafe, turn!"

I yanked the handlebars to the left and managed to miss the outhouse by an inch. Whew! That could have been a real mess. I zipped around the trailer and circled back. I knocked over a garbage can and scraped the backside off one of my snowmen. But no serious damage. This wasn't so hard, after all!

I looked over my shoulder at Uki. She gave me a big thumbs-up. And just like that, I was a certified snowmobile driver. I cranked the handlebars around and headed out across the tundra. Uki waved. Before long, the research center was just a speck in my rearview mirror. I felt my butt getting warm. Heated seat. Nice.

The first few miles were a piece of cake. Smooth and flat. I could feel my confidence building. I saw a herd of musk oxen straight ahead of me, hanging out like a polar street gang. I thought I was going to have to drive around them, but when I pressed my horn, they moved out of the way. Respect.

I guess that's when I got cocky.

Just ahead I saw a series of snowdrifts in a long row. I started to weave between them like a slalom skier. So much fun! Why had I been so nervous? I was *born* for this—Rider of the Frozen North! If only my family could see me now!

I pressed the throttle lever all the way down. I felt the snow spray up along the sides. Faster and faster. Then, all of a sudden, the snowmobile started to make weird noises. Spitting and sputtering noises. Instead of going faster and faster, it was going slower and slower. The engine gave one final cough, and then...it just stopped.

Uh-oh.

I realized that there was one little thing Uki had forgotten to point out. The gas gauge. I sure noticed it now. It was round with a red needle. And the red needle was pointing to "E."

I slid off my cozy seat onto the frozen tundra. I knew I was in big trouble. I was probably a hundred miles from the nearest gas station. The wolves would smell me any minute. I looked left. I looked right. Then I looked down.

Footprints! *Human* footprints.

Salvation!

CHAPTER 30

SCARED OUT OF MY SKIN

I was hoping the footprints would lead me to a cozy lodge. Or even better, a Christmas tree farm. But I'd been walking for about an hour and there was nothing around. And I mean *nothing*. This bleak and barren stuff was starting to get really old.

Then I saw it. Smoke! It was coming out of a small chimney that was peeking out from a little cove. That's where the footprints were leading. I picked up the pace. When I came around a big snowdrift, I saw a tiny shack. But this was no fairy tale cottage. It looked like it was made out of whale bones and walrus hide. All around the sides were drying animal skins. Sheepskins. Moose skins. Sealskins. Reindeer skins. Lemming skins. The shack had a rusty tin roof and lying on top of it

were a bunch of dried tusks and horns and antlers.
This place was an animal graveyard!

From inside the shack, I could hear heavy
metal music. *Really* heavy.

Maybe the Brain Bashers or the Horns of
Satan. Serious stuff.

I tiptoed up to the front of the shack. I stood on
the porch and leaned over to peek into the window.
It was small and the glass was grimy. I could make
out a potbellied stove inside. And right next to it
was a potbellied man. He was thrashing around to
the thrash music, using a caribou antler for an air
guitar. I angled my head for a better look. Then my
blood ran cold. I knew that face.

I had stumbled on the lair of Broacher the
Poacher!

Welcome to my nightmare!
Surrender to my gloom!
Pierce my heart of leather!
Feel the kiss of doom!

I had to get out of there! Slowly and quietly. Just like backing away from a bear den. I ducked down from the window and tiptoed off the porch. A loose board creaked. I froze. But then I realized there was no way Broacher could hear it over the music. I stepped off onto the snow and started hightailing it back out of the cove. I didn't get far.

CLANG!

I felt something snap shut on the heel of my left kamik like a steel trap. I looked down. It *was* a steel trap! Lucky for me, it was only a rabbit trap. Kind of like being nipped by a toy poodle. The bad news was the trap was attached to a chain. And the chain was attached to a metal spike. And the spike was frozen into the ground.

Suddenly, the heavy metal music got a lot louder. I looked back. The door to the shack was open! Broacher the Poacher was standing there with the caribou antler in his hand. His beady eyes looked in my direction. He stepped off the porch and headed right toward me. This was it. My time was up.

I was about to become just another hide on his wall.

CHAPTER 31

THE FRIGID FUGITIVE

Then my survival instincts kicked in. I yanked my left foot hard. No good. The chain was too strong. Broacher was getting closer, waving his antler like a baseball bat. I yanked again! This time my kamik came off with the trap still attached to it. I was free! For the moment.

I got up and started running in one kamik and one wool sock. Lucky for me, Broacher was not in great shape. Probably a smoker. I could hear him wheezing and puffing behind me as I ran around the snowdrift at the top of the cove, pausing to catch my breath.

As soon as I heard Broacher get close, I took off again across the tundra.

I twisted. I turned. I bobbed. I weaved. But I

couldn't shake him. What did I expect? He was an experienced wildlife tracker, with a high kill count. I looked everywhere for something to hide behind. A tree. A rock. A shrub. But as you know by now, the tundra is pretty much filled with nothing.

When I got to a stream bed, I thought about wading in. Nobody can track you through a stream. That's a proven fact. Escaped convicts use that trick all the time. But then I realized the stream would freeze me as solid as a Popsicle. Which would make me a lot easier to find. I heard Broacher's footsteps behind me. He was relentless. He was a machine. He was superhuman!

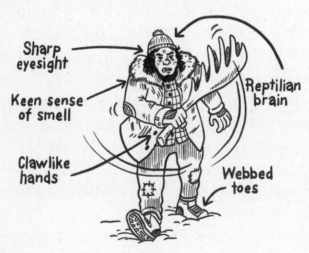

Sharp
eyesight

Keen sense
of smell

Clawlike
hands

Reptilian
brain

Webbed
toes

A few yards from the stream bank, the snow got even deeper. It was impossible to walk through, especially with only one kamik. I could hear Broacher getting closer. He was grunting and huffing. Getting madder by the minute, no doubt. I expected no mercy.

I took one more step and fell facedown in the snow. My arms sank in up to my elbows. I was about to give up when a spark went off in my brain. I started digging with my hands. Just like Panuk and Uki. I dug like my life depended on it! Before long, I was tucked into my own personal snow cave. I was safe!

Or was I?

It only took me another second to realize that even though I was hidden in my shelter, my tracks led right to it. Nice try, Rafe. For a master stalker like Broacher, I was a sitting duck. Sure enough, I heard his footsteps in the snow right outside my hideaway. He probably had his skinning knife ready.

Suddenly, I saw little flashes of fur pop out of the snow in front of my face. My digging had disturbed a family of pygmy shrews! They hopped right out of my snow cave and scurried across the snow like furry little raisins.

Broacher was so close I could hear him smacking his lips. But not for me.

Believe it or not, he started chasing the shrews! Maybe he considered them a delicacy. Or maybe he wanted to add their tiny skins to his collection. This was my chance!

I peeked out of the cave and saw Broacher running every which way across the tundra trying to catch the little critters with his bare hands.

I slipped out of my snow cave and ran off in the other direction, as fast as my one sock and one kamik could carry me. I ran as far as I could and then I started walking. More like limping. I was tired and wet and cold, but pretty soon I ran into my old snowmobile tracks and started following them back toward the research center. I put one freezing foot in front of the other, thinking about my close call—and how nature had saved me. I knew one thing for sure:

The pygmy shrew was my new favorite animal.

CHAPTER 32

RAFE WITH ALL THE TRIMMINGS

By the time I got back to the research center, my left sock was frozen solid. I was shivering. I was shuddering. My left foot felt like a giant ice cube, and my right foot wasn't much better. The lights from that little trailer were the most beautiful sight I'd ever seen. I pushed the door open and tripped over the doorsill. Not the most graceful entrance. But what do you expect from a guy with two numb feet? Everybody jumped up and rushed over to help me up.

"R-Rafe! Are y-you okay?" asked Penelope.

"What happened to your kamik?" asked Uki.

"Where's my snowmobile?" asked Panuk.

First things first. Dr. Deerwin took one look

at me and made me lie right down. She wrapped thermal foil blankets around me until I looked like a Thanksgiving turkey. Then she pulled off my frozen sock.

Hey! You forgot the stuffing!

"D-Don't w-worry," said Penelope. "M-My m-mom is an expert on injuries t-to the extremities!"

Naturally. Dr. Deerwin was an expert on *everything*. Right away, I knew my feet were in good hands. Dr. Deerwin held my heels up and checked things over. She poked my ankles and tapped my soles.

"It's not frostbite," she said. "Just frostnip."

That sounded like good news. At least she

wouldn't have to amputate anything. Dr. Deerwin gave Panuk a thermometer and told him to fill up a plastic tub with warm water—104 degrees Fahrenheit exactly. Then she lowered both of my feet into the tub and gave them a little rubdown to get the blood flowing.

She made a weird face, the kind you make when you feel something disgusting.

"Good gosh, Rafe," said Dr. Deerwin. "When was the last time you cut your toenails?"

I had to admit that it had been a while. Toe trimming was not my favorite personal care activity. Which is probably why my nails were all crusty and curled under.

Hills Village House of Horrors

Principal Stricker's pet tarantula

Farmer Frank's three-headed weasel

Mama Luccino's raw-snail pizza

Rafe Khatchadorian's toes

Walking around in snowshoes and tight kamaak for the past ten days probably hadn't helped. Dr. Deerwin looked over at Penelope.

"Get the clippers," she said. "We need to trim these monsters before he gets an infection."

Penelope pulled Dr. Deerwin's medical bag off a shelf and took out a tool that looked like it was designed for trimming animal claws. I hoped it had been disinfected. Penelope lifted my feet out of the water and went to work—one overgrown toenail at a time. So humiliating. I never wanted her to see me this way. As a distraction, I started gabbing.

As Penelope snipped away, I told everybody about my harrowing adventure. About Broacher's evil lair. About all the skins and tusks and horns and antlers. About being stalked across the tundra like a wild animal. About my narrow escape.

Penelope stopped in mid-snip. She looked up.

"D-Did Broacher have any p-p…?"

"No polar bear skins," I said. "Not yet anyway."

Everybody was pretty relieved about that. PB3 could still be out there somewhere, alive and kicking. Penelope finished her work and the feeling started to come back into my freshly trimmed toes. The bad news was, the research center was now short one snowmobile. And as for the Christmas tree search—obviously an epic fail.

So much for my perfect Tundra Christmas.

CHAPTER 33

PENCIL ME IN

As I warmed up in my foil wrapping, I saw something fluttering in front of my eyes. I thought it might be a side effect of frostnip, but then I realized it was Nuki. He was taking a few practice flights from one side of the trailer to the other. He still looked a little wobbly to me, but at least he made it back to his nest without crashing into anything.

"Nice landing, baby!" said Penelope. She was the world's best flight instructor.

Just before I turned in for the night, Dr. Deerwin slathered my feet with a thick white lotion. So soothing.

"It's udder cream," she said.

Okay, it sounded gross, but I figured if it was good enough for the underside of a cow, it was good enough for my ugly feet. Dr. Deerwin's masterful tootsie massage knocked me right out.

I was deep into a terrific dream about the Kris Kringle CookieFest back home when I felt a tap on my shoulder. I opened one eye. It was Penelope. She was leaning over me. She put her finger over her lips and pointed out the window next to my sleep pod. I opened the other eye and looked out. I blinked. I didn't see anything. And then…

There it was! The same strange light I'd seen a few nights ago. I hadn't been imagining it after all.

Penelope was holding her field notebook and a pencil.

What's that? she scribbled on an empty page.

I took the pencil and scribbled back, *No idea*. Actually, I had some theories, but they didn't make much sense. To be fair, I was still half asleep.

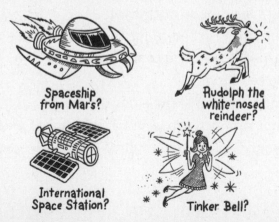

Spaceship from Mars?

Rudolph the white-nosed reindeer?

International Space Station?

Tinker Bell?

She grabbed the pencil back.

LET'S FIND OUT! she wrote, in all caps, underlined.

My feet were still coated in udder cream, but that actually made it easier to slip on my socks. We both put on our pants and parkas. We didn't zip up.

Not inside. Too much noise. We tiptoed to the door and opened it an inch at a time. When there was just enough of a gap, we slipped out and pressed the door shut. Once we were outside, we zipped up our parkas, pulled on our gloves, and strapped on our snowshoes. I was glad I'd packed an extra pair!

It was pitch-black outside the trailer. To the north, we could see the little glow that was Niksik. But out toward the Chukchi Sea where we'd seen the light, there was nothing. It could have been the end of the world out there. Sure looked like it.

I knew this was a bad idea. The tundra at night was no place for humans.

Definitely no place for a couple of middle school kids. I knew Dr. Deerwin would not approve. But right now I was just happy that Penelope had decided to wake *me* up instead of Panuk. And I realized that I'd follow her anywhere. Even with two creamy feet.

We started out in the direction of the sea. We walked for a mile without seeing anything. And then...

"Th-There it is!" said Penelope.

It was the same light again. We sped up. Our snowshoes made little crunching sounds in the snow. As we hiked along, we saw the light come and go, moving back and forth like a polar firefly. What the heck *was* it?? Wait! Could it be the Northern Lights?? I'd promised Grandma Dotty a picture and I didn't even have a camera.

By now the research center was way behind us. All around us was nothing but dark, empty tundra. Except for the hungry wolves that were no doubt watching us from a distance, waiting for the right moment to pounce. I was starting to feel nervous, and a little guilty. Penelope was a few steps ahead of me. I caught up and tapped her on the shoulder.

"We should probably go back," I said.

She turned around and looked at me like I was crazy.

"B-But we haven't s-solved the mystery," she said.

"I know," I said. "But it's dangerous out here. And I don't want to get into trouble with your mom again."

Penelope patted my parka sleeve.

"D-Don't worry. We'll be b-back before she w-wakes up," she said, "I p-promise."

I had my doubts about that. I knew for a fact that Dr. Deerwin was a very early riser.

"B-Besides, R-Rafe," said Penelope, "I always f-feel s-safe when I'm with you."

No fair. She had found my true weakness. How did she know I was a sucker for flattery?

CHAPTER 34

LET'S HEAR IT FOR THE ICEBERG!

By the time we got to the Chukchi shoreline, the light was nowhere to be seen. But now there was a little shimmer in the sky to the east—just slightly lighter than total blackness. In December up here, it's what passes for dawn. But at least it was enough for us to see the sea in front of us.

The water was even slushier than the last time we were there. And the ice chunks were even bigger. There was an iceberg floating in the distance that looked as big as Mount Rushmore, only without all the presidents.

"Let's g-go!" said Penelope.

At first, I was relieved. I thought she meant it was time to head back home.

Instead, she pulled off her snowshoes and jumped right off the shore onto a floating hunk of ice.

"What are you *doing*?" I yelled.

She pointed at the giant iceberg.

"Maybe if we climb to the top, we can see something!" she shouted back. She was already two ice floes out and heading for her third.

"Bad idea!" I yelled.

For once in my life, I actually felt like the voice of reason. But Penelope was too far out to hear me. What else could I do? I yanked off my snowshoes and followed her. As soon as I jumped, I realized that my feet weren't totally back to normal. Balancing on ice requires the agility of a cat. I had the agility of a musk ox. When my ice floe rocked, I almost fell headfirst into the choppy Chukchi.

Penelope was stretching the distance between us. I had to catch up! After another hop, slip, and a jump, I was getting closer. Now she was just a couple of floes away.

"Penelope!" I shouted. "Wait for me!"

Before I knew it, we were just one ice floe apart. There was a channel of dark water between us, filled with whitish-green slush.

"G-Grab my hand!" said Penelope. She leaned across the gap and stretched her arms out. I reached out and grabbed her gloves. I pushed off with both feet. She pulled back with both hands. I jumped from my floe to hers. My kamaak skidded as I landed. Penelope grabbed on to my parka and we both fell over onto the ice. I was freaked out, but Penelope was laughing. Pretty soon, I was laughing, too.

Strange. I knew this was the last place in the world we should be. But it was just so much fun to be with her. I can't really explain it. Once you feel it for yourself, you'll understand. Trust me, it feels like nothing else.

When we got to our feet, the iceberg was looming over us about twenty yards away. It was covered in layers and swirls with big pieces missing, like a leftover birthday cake.

"It's f-fantastic!" Penelope yelled across the water.

Her voice echoed against the iceberg.

Hey! I'm trying to hibernate here!

"Did you hear that?" I said.

She nodded. "S-So c-cool!"

"Listen to *this*!" I said. I clapped my gloves together. The echo came back loud and clear. *Clap!* This was fun! And I was just getting warmed up. I pulled off my gloves and stuffed them into my pockets. Then opened my arms as wide as they would go.

"Ready?" I said.

"G-Go for it!" said Penelope.

I brought my bare palms together with everything I had.

CLAP!

This time the echo came back with a little something extra—kind of a low rumble, followed by the sound of ice cracking.

"R-Rafe! L-Look!" Penelope shouted.

The whole side of the iceberg was collapsing! A piece the size of a city bus slid off the top and crashed into the water. A huge wave rippled out and headed right for us. Two seconds later, the wave hit our ice floe. I grabbed Penelope to keep from falling. Or maybe she grabbed me. Hard to remember. All I knew was that our ice floe was breaking free of all the other floes and moving away on its own. We were trapped. We were alone. And we were floating out to sea!

Nobody was clapping now.

CHAPTER 35

THE PERFECT LURE

Titanic is Grandma Dotty's favorite movie. I probably watched that DVD with her at least a hundred times. I knew every scene by heart.

That Leo is such a dollface!

So the situation at the moment actually seemed

pretty familiar—a boy and a girl trapped on a tiny slab in the middle of an endless ocean, with no hope in sight. But this was no movie. This was *us*!

The only good thing was that Penelope had wrapped herself around me to stay warm. That part was nice. But the thought of freezing together in the middle of the Chukchi Sea? Not good. Our eyelashes were frosted over. Our teeth were chattering. I thought about paddling with my hands, but I was afraid they might just freeze and fall off. Then I'd never be able to write my polar bear research report. Unless I learned how to type with my ugly toes. That would take years of training. I realized I wasn't making any sense. I felt like I was getting delirious. I thought I heard Celine Dion singing "My Heart Will Go On."

"R-Rafe, I s-see it!" Penelope whispered. She could barely move her lips. I raised my head and stared out over the water.

The light was back! Maybe it was a rescue ship. My heart jumped.

Then it sank. It was a ship, all right. But not the kind I was hoping for. Turns out the light we'd been chasing all night was on the crow's nest of

the *Grozny*! I didn't know which was worse, being
trapped on an ice floe, or being captured by evil
whalers. But we didn't have any choice.

We started hearing shouts and whistles from
the deck of the *Grozny*. The ship's horn blasted.
It sounded like a dying goose. And then the huge
rusty hull pulled up right alongside us. We heard
a loud *ffwapp* and saw a black cargo net drop over
the side. The crew was leaning over the rail and
yelling at us in Russian. Up close, they looked like
a pretty rough bunch.

I pushed Penelope toward the net. She grabbed
on. I grabbed on right next to her. I think they

expected us to scamper up like Navy SEALs, but we barely had enough strength to hold on. So they started hauling the net up with us attached, like two flies in a spiderweb.

When we got to the top, we tumbled over the rail and landed on the deck with a thud. We heard footsteps coming down the metal stairs from the wheelhouse. It was the captain! The sailors stepped aside as he stomped over and started shouting. Fortunately for us, Penelope had spent a Christmas in Kiev, so she understood some of what he was saying.

"His name is Captain Popov," she whispered. "He thinks we're spies from the Alaskan government. And he wants to use us for fish bait!"

How do I get myself into these pickles? I could have been home wrapping presents and sipping eggnog. Instead, I was lying on a cold metal deck waiting for somebody to dangle me on a fishhook. Then we heard another voice. This one was in English. Rough and mean.

"Not bait," the voice said. "Better to hold them for ransom. Kids this age fetch a pretty penny."

I looked up. It was Broacher the Poacher!

Our day just went from extremely bad to absolutely horrible.

CHAPTER 36

THE TIES THAT BIND

Two minutes later, Penelope and I were down in the galley of the ship. We were tied back-to-back with some pretty impressive nautical knots. When it came to rope, these sailors really knew their stuff.

The galley smelled like sweat and microwave pizza. The pine-scented air freshener wasn't helping. It just reminded me that I still hadn't found a Christmas tree. But, obviously, I had bigger things to worry about now.

We could hear Popov and Broacher up on deck arguing about how much ransom money to ask for us—and whether it should be in dollars or rubles. All of a sudden, we heard a shout from the lookout on the prow of the ship.

"Kit! Kit!"

Penelope recognized the word right away.

"Wh-Whale!"

The captain shouted something up to the wheelhouse. The ship made a sharp turn to starboard (that's toward the right). We rolled across the floor. The captain shouted something else. Then the ship turned to port (that's toward the left). We rolled back the other way.

My days working on boats at the Green Banks Resort had taught me a few seafaring terms. But all my knowledge wasn't keeping me from getting seasick. It seemed like the whale was doing some evasive maneuvers. Good for him. Bad for my belly. But I took a few deep breaths and rode it out. We heard the whole crew rushing toward the harpoon gun. There was a lot of clattering metal and grinding gears. Broacher was yelling to the crew.

"Remember," he said, "I showed you miserable sea dogs the route! That means I get half the whale oil!"

The thought of a big, beautiful whale being chopped into bits and pieces made me feel even sicker.

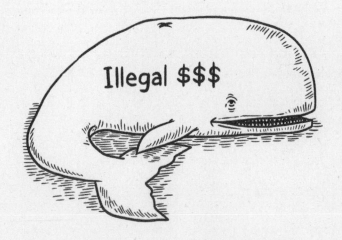

I started squirming and pulling against the ropes, but it only made the knots tighter.

"H-Hold still," whispered Penelope.

I stopped moving. I could feel the ropes cutting into my wrists and ankles.

They were so tight around my wrists that I

could hardly feel my hands. Then, suddenly, the ropes were loose! We were free!

I turned around. Penelope was smiling and holding up her oversized nail clippers.

"G-Good thing I f-forgot to put them b-back," she said.

CHAPTER 37

WHAT GOES UP...

We climbed the steps that led from the galley to the deck. I opened the hatch and took a peek. It was a madhouse out there! A bunch of sailors were crowded around the prow, looking through thick binoculars. Two sailors were loading a huge harpoon into the front of the harpoon gun. It looked like a giant spear with a shiny metal tip. Attached to the end was a long coil of yellow rope, hundreds and hundreds of feet of it. Strong enough to hold a whale, I guess.

The ship was rocking like a rubber duck. When the prow dipped, we could see the back of the whale in the distance. The crew started shouting even louder. The harpoon team started cranking the gun around.

"Dive, baby, dive!" Penelope whispered, like she was trying to contact the whale through mental telepathy. But she knew it was no use. The harpoon shooter took aim. Popov and Broacher were standing at the rail, rubbing their hands together. They had a big whale in their sights and two kids to ransom. It was probably looking like a very profitable day. They didn't notice us until...

"Noooooooooo!"

That was me, shouting at the top of my lungs. I shoved the hatch door open and jumped out on deck. I didn't have my sea legs, so I stumbled and slipped all over the place. I grabbed at the rail. I held on to the foremast. I braced myself against the capstan. Out of the corner of my eye, I could see Broacher reaching for his skinning knife. Was I scared? Sure. But I knew what I had to do. And I only had about one second to do it.

I jumped forward toward the harpoon gun just as the sailor started to pull the trigger. I slapped the backside of the black tube. The front end tipped up just as the harpoon shot out.

BANG!

Suddenly, everything was quiet. Popov and Broacher froze like statues.

The whole crew watched the harpoon fly up into the sky, pulling the yellow rope behind it. It went higher and higher. Then it started to fall back down like a missile.

Captain Popov's eyes opened wide. When he saw where the harpoon was about to land, he said what sounded like a very bad word.

I ran to the rail and looked out across the water. Another ship was coming out of the mist about a hundred yards away. There was no time for a warning. The harpoon was already coming down! Everybody watched as it dropped out of the sky and stabbed a big fat hole in the middle of the other ship's deck.

The ship looked brand-new. It was painted white and gray and I could read some big black lettering on the side.

It said US COAST GUARD.

CHAPTER 38

AN ARRESTING DEVELOPMENT

I guess it wasn't too hard to figure out where the harpoon came from. All they had to do was follow the rope.

Pretty soon, the deck of the *Grozny* was swarming with Coast Guard sailors in dark-blue uniforms. They seemed pretty annoyed about the hole in their deck. I guess they'd spent the whole morning polishing it. They brought along lots of handcuffs, enough for the whole *Grozny* crew.

Captain Popov tried to claim political immunity, but the Coast Guard captain wasn't buying it. Broacher said they were just fishing for trout, but that didn't fly, either. Besides, there were two reliable eyewitnesses.

"I'm Rafe Khatchadorian," I said to the Coast

Guard captain, "and this is my friend Penelope Deerwin. We saw everything."

"R-Rafe is a h-hero!" said Penelope. Then she told the whole story. Every last detail. I have to say, the Coast Guard captain was pretty impressed. I could see his assistant writing it all down for the official report. I checked to make sure they spelled my name right. Nobody ever does.

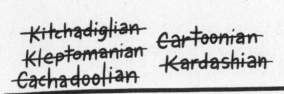

~~Kitchadiglian~~ ~~Cartoonian~~
~~Kleptomanian~~ ~~Kardashian~~
~~Cachadoolian~~
_____
Name

As the Coast Guard guys started searching the *Grozny* for contraband, I walked with Penelope to the prow of the ship. Off in the distance, we saw the whale surface and blow an extra big spout. I don't speak whale, but to me it looked like he was saying, "Thanks, dude!" That felt great.

"I'm r-really p-proud of you!" said Penelope.

That felt even better. But the feeling didn't last.

Obviously, I was happy the whale got away, and I was glad to see the *Grozny* crew and Broacher in chains. But I still got a sad little twinge deep inside. Because I realized that it was the day before Christmas.

And I had absolutely nothing to show for it.

CHAPTER 39

RIDING HIGH

A few minutes later, I was feeling a little better. There's nothing like a ride in an official Coast Guard helicopter to lift your spirits. In fact, it might just be the coolest thing in the world. Especially compared to being trapped on a floating piece of ice. We took off from a big platform on the deck of the Coast Guard ship and pretty soon we were a thousand feet up, looking out the open doors on both sides. Best view *ever*!

Penelope and I were each strapped in tighter than a baby in a car seat. The crew even loaned us helmets. The air was really cold, and it was too loud to talk, but I didn't care. I was loving every minute.

From that high up, we could see all the way

north to where the sea was solid ice—the way
Mother Nature intended. We could see Niksik in
the distance. It looked like a toy town. We could
even see the street where Panuk and Uki lived.
When we flew over the tundra, we saw a few arctic
foxes diving for cover under the snow. We probably
looked like the biggest bird of prey they'd ever
seen.

The helicopter made a dip and a turn and I got
the kind of feeling in my stomach you get when
you go over the top on a roller coaster. My heart

was beating a mile a minute. I looked over at Penelope to see if she was nervous.

No way. She was smiling from ear to ear. We could hear the pilot talking to the copilot through the speakers in our helmets.

"*Eyes on target,*" he said. "*Banking left twenty degrees.*"

"*Roger that,*" said the copilot. I bet these guys were really good at video games.

A few seconds later, a little speck came into view. The research center! The helicopter dipped lower and lower and the trailer got bigger and bigger.

When we swooped down to land, the wind from the propeller blew the roof right off the outhouse. Luckily, it was unoccupied at the moment.

The skids touched down on the snow right out front of the trailer. Dr. Deerwin came out and headed straight toward us. I could tell from the way she was walking that she was really mad. I'm sure the Coast Guard radioed ahead to expect us, but that just gave her more time to think up suitable punishments. I had a feeling I'd be the one fixing the outhouse.

The chopper engine turned off. The blades slowed down. The crew unstrapped us and took their helmets back. We hopped out of the door and dropped feetfirst onto the snow.

Dr. Deerwin was standing with her arms folded the way grown-ups do when you know you're in big trouble. Grounded-for-a-month trouble. Taking-away-your-phone trouble. But before she could say a single word, the helicopter pilot walked over and put his hands on our shoulders.

"Ma'am, I want you to know that you've got two brave kids here," he said. "You should be very proud."

I could tell the pilot made an impression on Dr. Deerwin. It didn't hurt that he looked a lot like the guy who plays Thor in the *Avengers* movies. Dr. Deerwin unfolded her arms.

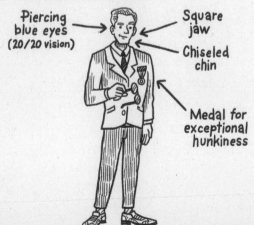

Piercing blue eyes (20/20 vision)

Square jaw

Chiseled chin

Medal for exceptional hunkiness

"What in heaven's name *happened* out there?" she asked.

The pilot gave Dr. Deerwin the whole rundown. A blow-by-blow description. Pretty dramatic. Then he turned toward me and Penelope. I thought he was about to shake our hands or pat us on the back. But he didn't. He snapped to attention and gave us a salute.

When Thor headed back to the chopper, Dr. Deerwin just stood there for a few seconds without saying anything. Then she pulled us both in tight and gave us the world's longest hug.

CHAPTER 40

IF YOU LOVE HIM,
LET HIM GO

Once the thrill of the chopper ride wore off, the holiday blues came back big-time. It was only a few hours until Christmas Eve. But instead of decorating a festive tree, I was nailing the top back onto the plastic outhouse. I heard the trailer door squeak and saw Penelope step outside. She was holding something in her hands tight against her chest. It was Nuki, the left-behind tern.

"It's okay, baby," Penelope was saying. "Don't be afraid."

I got down off the ladder and walked over. When I got closer, I could see that Penelope had tears in her eyes. She tried to pretend that it was just from the cold air, but she couldn't fool me.

"What's going on?" I asked.

Penelope looked down at Nuki, then up at me. "It's t-time for him to g-go," she said.

Now the tears made sense. I guess we all knew this day had to come. I'd watched Nuki getting healthier and plumper since we'd rescued him. His test flights in the trailer had gotten longer and stronger. Now his wing was totally healed. Penelope had been feeding him extra scraps of blubber over the past couple of days to build his strength. That stuff really works, by the way. I'm starting to think blubber is a miracle food.

Buy one, get one free! Works for warts, hair loss, and constipation. Not necessarily in that order!

As soon as Nuki got a feel for the outdoors, he started chirping and flapping. He was *very* excited. I pulled off one of my gloves and gave his head a little rub. I silently forgave him for the time he pooped on my parka. No hard feelings, my feathered friend.

Penelope took a few steps forward and turned her face toward the wind. She lifted Nuki up as high as she could and opened her palm.

"Go, baby, go!" she said.

Nuki took one hop on Penelope's wrist, then spread his wings and took off. He swooped down almost to the ground and then flapped hard to gain altitude. He rose higher and higher and then did a slow turn, coming back our way. When he was about fifty feet up, he started making slow circles around the research center. I started to worry. Maybe he was disoriented after all his time indoors. Maybe all his natural instincts were gone.

"Is he lost?" I asked.

"N-No," said Penelope. "He's s-saying g-good-bye."

Sure enough, after wiggling his wings at us a

couple of times, Nuki straightened out and headed due south.

"Say hi to Antarctica!" Penelope yelled.

"Merry Christmas!" I added. We both waved.

Some Christmas. At least Nuki got what he wanted. He was on his way home to his flock. Meanwhile, I was stuck with no tree, no lights, no presents, no cookies. All my efforts to create the perfect Tundra Christmas had failed. And now Penelope was as sad as I was, because she just lost her little buddy. This was turning out to be the worst Christmas Eve in holiday history.

Then, just as Nuki disappeared into the distance, Panuk and Uki popped out of the trailer, all cheerful and chipper.

"Let's go!" Panuk yelled. "It's time for *Quviasukvik!*" I had no idea what *Quviasukvik* was. I was afraid that it might be another one of Panuk's recipes for fermented fish. Take it from me, that's definitely an acquired taste. Then Dr. Deerwin came out. She was wearing a fake fur hat with sprigs of holly sticking out. Penelope cracked a little smile.

"M-Mom wears that h-hat every Ch-Christmas," she said. "No m-matter where w-we are!"

I was finished with fixing the outhouse, so I put my tools in the toolshed and used a little hand sanitizer to clean up. Uki was so excited she was practically jumping up and down.

"Let's go!" she said. "We can't be late!"

Panuk hopped into the driver's seat of the Jeep and turned on the engine. We all piled in—Dr. Deerwin riding shotgun as usual, with me, Penelope, and Uki crammed into the backseat.

"Seat belts, everybody!" said Dr. Deerwin. And then we were off, bouncing across the frozen tundra.

"Where are we going?" I asked.

"Where do you *think*?" said Panuk, as if I'd just asked the stupidest question in the world.

"Quviasukvik is our big winter holiday," said Uki. "And holiday means *home*!"

CHAPTER 41

LIFE OF THE PARTY

Twenty bouncy minutes later, we pulled up in front of the family house in Niksik. I couldn't believe my eyes. It was decorated from top to bottom with Christmas lights! There was even an inflatable Santa out front—about fifteen feet tall. They had it standing up on a pile of crates so the huskies wouldn't chew through it, which made it look even more impressive.

Just seeing all the Christmas trappings gave me a warm feeling inside, even if I was thousands of miles from Hills Village.

"You g-guys celebrate Ch-Christmas?" asked Penelope.

"Of *course!*" said Panuk.

"Christmas *and* Quviasukvik," said Uki. "Two holidays for the price of one!"

We could see steam on the windows, and no wonder—when we opened the door, there were even more people inside than the last time we visited. And the decibel level was off the charts.

Tonight it was mostly relatives. Grandparents,

208

moms, dads, uncles, aunts, and *tons* of little nieces and nephews.

There were logs crackling in the fireplace and stockings hanging from the mantel. And over in one corner there was a Christmas tree—so tall the tip was bent up against the ceiling. I could smell the scent of spruce from all the way across the room. Panuk and Uki's mom elbowed her way through the crowd to greet us.

"*Quyanaq Kaigavsi!*" she said. "Welcome!"

There was barely room to take off our parkas, let alone hang them up. So we just dropped them by the door. Dr. Deerwin started to mingle and the rest of us formed kind of a human train to move through the throng, with Panuk leading the way. The smallest cousins squealed and climbed all over Uki as soon as they saw her. I guess she was everybody's favorite babysitter.

When we finally reached the table at the other end of the room, it was loaded with traditional Quviasukvik treats—roast caribou and fish, sweet berries and flatbread, and yep, blubber. Also strawberry pudding and a cookie assortment that would do Grandma Dotty proud. I saw one of the little kids dipping into some kind of pink foamy dessert. It looked so good I decided to skip the main course.

"What's that?" I asked Uki.

"*Agutuk*," she said. "Aka Inuit ice cream." She scooped a big helping into a bowl for me. "Try it!"

I grabbed a spoon and dug right in. It was smooth and sweet, and a little salty, too. Different—but tasty.

"What's *in* this?" I asked between bites. I didn't want to be a pig, but it was really good. Secretly, I was thinking about selling the recipe to Ben & Jerry's.

"Let's see…" said Uki, ticking off the ingredients on her fingers. "Berries…sugar…snow…seal oil… and reindeer fat!" I put my spoon down.

One thing I've learned about Inuit food is that it's full of surprises. And sometimes it's better not to ask too many questions. I handed the rest of my *agutuk* to a little kid with a Wormhole T-shirt. He slurped it up in two seconds. Suddenly I felt a pair of big hands clamp down on my shoulders.

"Rafe! Is that you?"

I turned around. It was Uncle Tarkik, and he

had the biggest grin on his face. He grabbed me and gave me a manly hug.

"Tell me!" he said. "Is it true??"

"Oh, it's true!" said Uki.

Turns out that the whole town of Niksik was buzzing about the *Grozny* incident. They'd all heard about how my derring-do with the harpoon gun had helped the whale escape. And for the Inuit people, protecting a whale is like protecting a sacred spirit.

A bunch of Uncle Tarkik's fishing pals crowded around me, shaking my hand and squeezing my muscles. A couple of them put their heads together and whispered. After a few seconds, they all nodded.

"*Tomgarsuk*," the oldest one said, putting his gnarly hand on my head.

I figured it meant something like "nice work," but Uki told me that I'd just been given an honorary Inuit name. Which was a pretty big deal for a skinny white kid from Hills Village.

"*Tomgarsuk* means Sky God," she said. I liked the sound of that. I thought it would look great on a baseball cap.

But before I could practice pronouncing it, the center of the living room started to clear and the crowd divided into two sides. Everybody started stamping their feet and waving their arms and shouting at the people across the room.

A minute ago, everybody had been so friendly.

Now it looked like there was about to be a big fight—a rumble on the tundra!

CHAPTER 42

I'M PULLING FOR YOU

I saw that the kids were out front on each side, staring each other down. Panuk was standing in front of the group on the right side of the room. Uki was standing in front of the group on the left. The grown-ups were crowded behind them, split into two big cheering sections.

Uncle Tarkik pulled a thick rope out of a chest and stretched it across the room between the two sides. Panuk and his team grabbed one end. Uki and her team grabbed the other.

"W-What's g-going on?" asked Penelope.

Uncle Tarkik gave us the lowdown.

"It's an ancient Quviasukvik tradition," he said. "A tug-of-war between the children born in the summer and the children born in the winter—the *aggirn* versus the *axigirn*." He looked down at me and Penelope.

"What are you waiting for?" he said. "Join your side!"

I was a June baby, so I headed for Uki's team. Penelope went over to the other side. I realized that I didn't even know her birthday. I hoped she wasn't faking her birth season just to be on Panuk's team. I slipped in behind Uki and grabbed the rope. Uncle Tarkik raised his hand in the air. Everybody waited for the signal. He dropped his hand, and the battle began!

The rope got stretched tight as the teams pulled from both sides. Panuk was strong right out of the gate. No surprise. He'd probably been practicing all year long. I could see Penelope gritting her teeth and bracing her feet on the floor. But Uki was tougher than she looked, and her technique was solid. She wrapped the rope around her waist for more traction and barked orders like a general storming the beach.

"Pull *together*!" she yelled. "Now!"

We all put our backs into it, but some of the kids on our team were so short that their little legs were dangling off the floor. They weren't really pulling. They were just along for the ride.

The rope went back and forth. A few feet this way, then a few feet that way. The grown-ups were yelling advice like parents at a soccer tournament, and I'm pretty sure there was some betting going on.

Panuk was getting red in the face, leaning back with all his might. I could tell he really wanted to win. So did Penelope. She hated to lose at anything.

"P-Pull harder!" I heard her shout. That seemed to give Panuk an extra burst of energy.

Just when I thought we were done for, a couple of beefy *aggirn* cousins joined our side. Uki shouted the cue and we all gave one final heave, pulling back with everything we had. Panuk's team went sprawling face-first onto the floor. I fell backward and knocked my head against the food table. When I heard dishes dropping, I ducked. And just in time. I almost got a faceful of *agutuk*.

"Go, Team Aggirn!" shouted Uki, pumping her fists over her head. Everybody cheered. Even Panuk and Penelope.

I was wondering if we'd get a trophy or a ribbon, but I guess the only prize these days was bragging rights for the whole year. Still, it felt good to be on a winning team for once in my life. Even if nobody actually picked me.

Historical Rewards for Tug-of-War Victory:

- Ice-Fishing Rights
- Walrus-Tusk Desk Set
- Wolf Repellent
- Mink Underpants
- Snowshoe Lessons

After the big event, the crowd filled up the room again and people headed to the food table for more goodies. I saw Dr. Deerwin digging into a dish of berry cobbler. She was about a foot taller than anybody else in the room and the only one with holly sticking out of her hat. She was hard to miss.

Suddenly, there was a loud knock on the door.

I figured it was probably the fire marshal. No question this party was a major violation. You couldn't fit another relative in here with a shoehorn.

"I'll get it," shouted Uncle Tarkik.

He twisted his way through the crowd until he got to the front of the room. He pulled the door open.

I almost fainted.

CHAPTER 43

GUESS WHO?

Well, I guess I didn't need to bring my own cookies!"

I couldn't believe my eyes.

It was Grandma Dotty! And right behind her was my mom! And my sister Georgia! And my dog Junior! They were all dressed up in holiday sweaters and caps. Except for Junior. He was wearing a set of fake antlers and a bright-red collar.

My heart was racing so fast I thought I might explode. I ran over and gave my mom a huge hug. There was a little tear in my eye but I tried not to show it.

I'd missed her so much! When I hugged Grandma Dotty, I almost crushed the cookie platter she was holding. When I let go, Georgia was standing right in front of me. Generally speaking, Georgia is not the hugging type, especially when it comes to me, her annoying older brother. She put her hands on her hips and looked me right in the eye.

"I've got one question for you, mister," she said. "Did you really save a whale?"

I nodded. The whole crowd cheered and started chanting, "*Tomgarsuk, Tomgarsuk!*"

That did it. Georgia gave me the biggest hug ever. Then Junior jumped up and started licking my face.

Hey, humans! If you love animals, why not pick up the first book written by a dog? Namely me! Perfect stocking stuffer!

After that, there were *kunik*s and introductions all around. Georgia took an instant liking to Panuk, of course. He was a total chick magnet.

Before I knew it, they were sharing a plate of Baffin berries and she was telling him all about her all-girl rock band. Grandma Dotty really hit it off with Uki and Panuk's mom. I could see them across the room comparing cookie recipes.

"How did you guys even *get* here?" I asked my mom.

"Thank Dr. Deerwin for that," she said.

It turned out that with all her world travels, Dr. Deerwin was pretty well connected with the US State Department. And I guess for the family of a certified whale rescuer, it wasn't that hard to arrange the trip, all expenses paid.

I really owed Dr. Deerwin. She'd already changed my life with everything she'd taught me about animals and nature. And now she even managed a Khatchadorian family reunion.

Suddenly the room started to settle down. I wondered if there was going to be another test of strength, but this looked like something else. Uki was gathering all the Inuit kids in front of the Christmas tree, tallest kids in back, shortest in front. All the grown-ups looked at one another and smiled. Lots of elbow nudging. Then they got very

220

quiet. I think they knew what was coming.

Uki took a breath and brushed the hair back from her face. Then she took a step forward and started singing. Clear and beautiful. After the first verse, the other kids joined in. I guess it was a traditional Quviasukvik carol. And from the look of the adults in the room, it was a real tearjerker. Not a dry eye in the house. Of course, Mom and I couldn't understand a word. But I could tell she was very impressed. Especially with Uki.

"That girl could be the next Celine Dion," she whispered. The ultimate compliment.

As soon as the song was finished, everybody whistled and clapped. In the middle of the applause, there was another knock on the door. Definitely the fire marshal this time, I thought.

Wrong again.

It was the polar ranger, the same guy who'd warned us all about the return of the *Grozny*. He was holding an official-looking piece of paper and an envelope in his hand.

"Is there a Rafe Khatchadorian here?" he called out. He butchered the pronunciation, but there was no doubt who he was looking for. Was I under arrest for the missing snowmobile? Was I guilty of illegal ice-floe riding? I decided to step forward and face the music.

"That's me," I said.

I felt Panuk and Uki and Penelope step up beside me. They weren't going to let me go down alone. Or at least maybe they'd visit me in prison. The polar ranger stared at me.

"Are you familiar with a federal fugitive named Vincent Elmo Broacher?" he asked.

How could I forget? Even his name gave me a shiver. I nodded.

"Are you aware that there is a reward for his capture?" the polar ranger asked. A reward? I flashed back to the wanted poster in the trailer. I remembered Broacher's face and the dead-or-alive part, but the rest was kind of a blur. The polar ranger reached into the envelope.

"Rafe Khatchadorian," he said, "I am pleased to inform you that as the individual primarily responsible for the apprehension of Mr. Broacher, you are hereby entitled to a reward in the amount of ten thousand dollars."

Everybody gasped. The polar ranger handed me the check. I couldn't believe it.

They even spelled my name right.

CHAPTER 44

WRAPPING UP

What a night. By the time the festivities wound down, it was way past my bedtime. We all gathered outside as the guests headed off through the streets of Niksik. So many people slapped me on the back on the way out that I was getting sore between the shoulder blades. Then Georgia heard something in the distance. Her ears perked up.

"Listen!" she said. "What's that?"

It was the sound of jingle bells. She looked at me with her eyes wide open.

"Don't get your hopes up," I said.

Sure enough, it was the dudes on the dogsled again, coming out of the darkness at the edge of town.

"Which way to Koyuk?" asked the guy with the longest beard.

Penelope just shook her head. They'd been going around in circles this whole time. *Arctic* circles. The other dude pointed back behind the sled.

"By the way," he said, "did anybody lose a snowmobile?"

Panuk ran over to the sled and did a little happy dance. Because tied behind it on a long rope was his pride and joy.

"We found it about ten miles back," said the dude. "Looks like some moron ran out of gas."

Okay. I deserved that. But the important thing was, I hadn't really *lost* the snowmobile after all. It had just been resting in the snow for a few days. And now it was back, safe and sound. It was a Tundra Christmas Miracle!

Penelope took the time to help the dudes out by drawing a little map in the snow.

Where You Are

Where You Should Be

Meanwhile, Panuk offered to give Georgia a ride back to the research center on his snowmobile. I could see right away that Mom had her doubts about that idea, so I put in a good word.

"Don't worry, Mom," I said. "Panuk's a really safe driver."

Panuk gave me a little nod. Then he pulled two spare helmets out of the back of the Jeep. He strapped his helmet on first and helped Georgia with hers. And then...off they went. I hadn't seen my sister so happy since she found out she was skipping fourth grade.

Dr. Deerwin got behind the wheel of the Jeep, with Mom and Grandma Dotty squeezed into the passenger seat beside her. The rest of us crowded into the back. By now, everybody was so wiped out we were using each other for pillows. Junior fell asleep against Penelope. Penelope fell asleep against Uki. Uki fell asleep against me.

I was pretty exhausted, too. But really happy. I had my whole family around me and a bunch of new friends. Not to mention a ten-thousand-dollar check in my pocket. As Christmas Eves go, this one turned out to be a real winner.

CHAPTER 45

SKY'S THE LIMIT

If you had told me that eight people could sleep in the research center trailer, I would have said you were nuts. But Panuk and Uki gave up their bunks to Mom and Grandma Dotty. Then they pulled out some extra sleeping bags so all of us youngsters could sleep on the floor. We were kind of like sardines in a can, but it all worked out. Take it from me, when you're really tired, you can sleep almost anywhere. I closed my eyes and conked out.

Temporarily.

I don't know what made me wake up at two a.m. At first, I thought it was the sound of Grandma Dotty's snoring. Then I realized it was the sound of her *not* snoring. When I opened my eyes and looked around, I could see shapes in all the sleep pods except hers.

Grandma Dotty was *gone*!

I wriggled out of my sleeping bag and felt my way around the whole trailer from top to bottom. No Grandma. I pulled on my kamaak and parka and ran to the outhouse. I banged on the door. No reply. I looked out across the tundra and saw a dark shape silhouetted against the snow.

"Grandma!" I shouted. Who else could it be? I panicked. I had to get to her before the wolves did.

As I ran toward her, something really weird started to happen. The sky began to glow like the goop in a lava lamp. It was swirly and green with rays shooting down toward the ground. It looked like an alien invasion. I ran even faster. Back off, extraterrestrials! Nobody abducts Grandma Dotty on my watch!

When I got to her, Grandma was standing quietly on the snow. She was wearing Dr. Deerwin's kamaak and parka, and she had one of Panuk's Inuit blankets wrapped around her for extra insulation.

"Grandma!" I said. "What's going on? You can't be out here."

She put her arm around me and faced the horizon.

"Isn't it beautiful?" she said.

Now the green in the sky was mixed with blue. Now purple. Now yellow. It looked like one of my mom's abstract paintings, except it was about a hundred miles wide. I was waiting for the alien spaceships to emerge any second. At least they'd take me and Grandma together.

"I've been waiting to see this my whole life," Grandma said.

That's when I got it. Of course. Duh.

The Northern Lights!

"Well," said Grandma, "that's one more thing off my bucket list."

CHAPTER 46

ALL ABOARD THE BIG BIRD

Christmas morning. Homeward bound.

We were standing on a huge stretch of tundra outside town. But this time there was no rickety puddle-jumper waiting for us. Instead, we were staring up at the biggest plane I'd ever seen in my life, courtesy of the US Coast Guard.

It turned out that the *Grozny* wasn't just poaching whales. It was also smuggling fur coats, seal pelts, and bootleg Zoom Cola. It was one of the biggest busts in Coast Guard history. So they figured sending a massive cargo plane to fly six people and a dog back to Hills Village was the least they could do.

The plane was a thirty-eight-ton LC-130 Hercules transport, the kind they use to fly

Things That Would Fit
Inside This Plane:
☑ Whale
☑ ⅔ of Swifty's Diner
☑ School bus
☑ Entire research center

supplies into the science station in Antarctica.
It could land and take off from pretty much
anywhere on the planet. I only know that because
one of the crew members told us. He seemed pretty
proud of his aircraft, and I could see why. This
thing was taller than any building in Niksik. It
had four huge propellers and a hatch in the back
big enough to drive a truck through. The rear
ramp was down and we could see the huge space
inside—like a cave that went on forever.

The entire population of the town came out
to see us off. All two hundred of them. Plus their
huskies. There were hugs and nose rubs all
around. Panuk and Uki's mom gave Grandma
Dotty a platter of homemade cookies for the ride,
along with her favorite Inuit recipes. And Uncle
Tarkik gave me a carving of my head made from
whalebone. Excellent likeness.

"Good luck, Tomgarsuk!" he said. Then he gave me another manly hug.

Personally, I thought Panuk's good-byes to Penelope and Georgia were taking a little too long, so I gave Uki an extra *kunik* to even things out. I told her that she was a really great singer and that I couldn't wait to stream her on Spotify.

Then it was time to go. I headed up the ramp with Mom, Grandma Dotty, Dr. Deerwin, Penelope, Georgia, and Junior. We gave our final waves to everybody outside. The crew strapped us into our seats—custom made and heated, just like the seat on Panuk's snowmobile. When the giant hatch closed behind us, the whole inside of the plane lit up with twinkly red and green lights. Then the door from the cockpit opened. Out stepped a chubby guy with a red flight suit and a white beard.

"Merry Christmas, everybody!" he said. "I'm Captain Claus, and I'll be your pilot today."

Nice touch.

When the Hercules took off, it sounded like a freight train. But once we got airborne, it flew as smooth as udder cream. Captain Claus did a little fly-around and dipped his wings to the crowd below. Everybody waved.

Then, just like Nuki, we headed south.

THE END

THERE'S MORE...

That last page *would* be a logical place to wrap up the story, but that would leave a few loose ends. I don't know about you, but I *hate* loose ends.

For one thing, you're probably wondering about that ten-thousand-dollar reward check in my pocket. I'd thought about it a lot. And in my mind, it was already spent. After all, it *was* Christmas. And everybody had been really, really good. So I'd made up a list of very personal presents, and it went like this:

My mom was going to get a weekend painting course—in Paris.

Georgia was getting the new electric guitar and Mega-Blaster amp she'd been drooling over.

Grandma Dotty was getting a new convection oven, ideal for cookie baking.

Panuk and Uki were getting a research trailer renovation, complete with indoor plumbing.

Of course, I wasn't totally selfless. I'd decided to treat myself to a deluxe game console and every version of Wormhole ever made.

That left Penelope. I hadn't picked out her gift yet. It had to be really special. All I knew is that it would have something to do with wings. And feathers.

I felt Junior nuzzling my leg from the seat next to mine. Considering it was his second plane flight ever, he was taking the experience pretty well. From the next row back, I heard Dr. Deerwin telling Penelope that they could stay home for Christmas from now on, no matter what. I did a private fist pump. That meant I could invite them to the Kris Kringle CookieFest! Mom and Grandma Dotty were already fast asleep. I could see that Georgia was busy calculating the plane's speed and fuel consumption.

That left me pretty much alone with my thoughts about the expedition. Which were mostly good. Of course, we only found two out of three adult polar bears, but the two cubs were an unexpected bonus. I'd escaped certain death a few times. I learned that I function well in a subzero, low-light environment. And I was no longer intimidated by harpoons or lemmings.

I could feel the plane making a gentle turn.

We were flying really low, way below the clouds.
I looked out one of the windows the Coast Guard
added just for us. Everything below was white and
flat and still.

Except for one thing.

One very *big* thing.

Was it *possible*??

I leaned over and pressed my face against the
window for a better look. I squinted. Sure enough.
There he was, moving slowly across the tundra.
Noble. Proud. And collar-free. I thought about
shouting out to everybody else. Then I decided to
keep it just between the two of us.

Happy Quviasukvik, PB3!

THE END (FOR REAL)

READ THE MIDDLE SCHOOL SERIES

Find out more:
www.penguin.co.uk

THE
MIDDLE
SCHOOL
SERIES

THE WORST YEARS OF MY LIFE
(with Chris Tebbetts)
This is the insane story of my first year at middle school,
when I, Rafe Khatchadorian, took on a real-life bear (sort of),
sold my soul to the school bully, and fell for the most popular
girl in school. Come join me, if you dare…

GET ME OUT OF HERE!
(with Chris Tebbetts)
We've moved to the big city, where I'm going to a super-fancy
art school. The first project is to create something based on
our exciting lives. But my life is TOTALLY BORING.
It's time for Operation Get a Life.

MY BROTHER IS A BIG, FAT LIAR
(with Lisa Papademetriou)
So you've heard all about my big brother, Rafe, and now it's
time to set the record straight. (Almost) EVERYTHING he
says is a Big, Fat Lie. I'm Georgia, and it's time for some
payback…Khatchadorian style.

HOW I SURVIVED BULLIES, BROCCOLI, AND SNAKE HILL
(with Chris Tebbetts)
I'm excited for a fun summer at camp—until I find out it's a summer *school* camp. There's no fun and games here, just a whole lotta trouble!

ULTIMATE SHOWDOWN
(with Julia Bergen)
Who would have thought that we—Rafe and Georgia—would ever agree on anything? That's right—we're writing a book together. And the best part? We want you to be part of the fun too!

SAVE RAFE!
(with Chris Tebbetts)
I'm in worse trouble than ever! I need to survive a gut-bustingly impossible outdoor excursion so I can return to school next year. But will I get through in one piece?

JUST MY ROTTEN LUCK
(with Chris Tebbetts)
I'm heading back to Hills Village Middle School, but only if I take "special" classes... If that wasn't bad enough, when I somehow land a place on the school football team, I find myself playing alongside the biggest bully in school, Miller the Killer!

DOG'S BEST FRIEND
(with Chris Tebbetts)
It's a dog-eat-dog world. When I started my own dog-walking empire, I didn't think it could go so horribly wrong! Somehow, I always seem to end up in deep doo-doo...

ESCAPE TO AUSTRALIA
(with Martin Chatterton)
I just won an all-expenses paid trip of a lifetime
to Australia. But here's the bad news: I MIGHT NOT
MAKE IT OUT ALIVE!

FROM HERO TO ZERO
(with Chris Tebbetts)
I'm going on the class trip of a lifetime! What could
possibly go wrong? I've spent all of middle school being
chased by Miller the Killer, but on this trip, there's
NOWHERE TO RUN!

BORN TO ROCK
(with Chris Tebbetts)
My brother, Rafe Khatchadorian, has been public enemy
#1 my whole life. But if I want to win the Battle
of the Bands, I'm going to have to recruit the most
devious person I know...

MASTER OF DISASTER
(with Chris Tebbetts)
My buddy Jimmy and I are throwing a huge festival
dedicated to BOOKS! But when one tiiiiiny problem
snowballs into a BIG one, everyone's gotta work together
so the party doesn't get shut down—PERMANENTLY!

FIELD TRIP FIASCO
(with Martin Chatterton)
GUESS WHERE I'M GOING? ON AN ALL-
EXPENSES-PAID ART TRIP TO CALIFORNIA!
And this time, nothing's going to go wrong!
Famous last words, right?

IT'S A ZOO IN HERE

(with Brian Sitts)

I got a summer job at the zoo! This has got to be better than school, right? Especially with a lion needing my help...

ALSO BY JAMES PATTERSON

MIDDLE SCHOOL SERIES

The Worst Years of My Life (*with Chris Tebbetts*)
Get Me Out of Here! (*with Chris Tebbetts*)
My Brother Is a Big, Fat Liar (*with Lisa Papademetriou*)
How I Survived Bullies, Broccoli, and Snake Hill (*with Chris Tebbetts*)
Ultimate Showdown (*with Julia Bergen*)
Save Rafe! (*with Chris Tebbetts*)
Just My Rotten Luck (*with Chris Tebbetts*)
Dog's Best Friend (*with Chris Tebbetts*)
Escape to Australia (*with Martin Chatterton*)
From Hero to Zero (*with Chris Tebbetts*)
Born to Rock (*with Chris Tebbetts*)
Master of Disaster (*with Chris Tebbetts*)
Field Trip Fiasco (*with Martin Chatterton*)
It's a Zoo in Here! (*with Brian Sitts*)

ALI CROSS SERIES

Ali Cross
Ali Cross: Like Father, Like Son
Ali Cross: The Secret Detective

I FUNNY SERIES

I Funny (*with Chris Grabenstein*)
I Even Funnier (*with Chris Grabenstein*)
I Totally Funniest (*with Chris Grabenstein*)
I Funny TV (*with Chris Grabenstein*)
School of Laughs (*with Chris Grabenstein*)
The Nerdiest, Wimpiest, Dorkiest I Funny Ever
(*with Chris Grabenstein*)

MAX EINSTEIN SERIES

The Genius Experiment (*with Chris Grabenstein*)
Rebels with a Cause (*with Chris Grabenstein*)
Saves the Future (*with Chris Grabenstein*)
World Champions! (*with Chris Grabenstein*)

TREASURE HUNTERS SERIES
Treasure Hunters (*with Chris Grabenstein*)
Danger Down the Nile (*with Chris Grabenstein*)
Secret of the Forbidden City (*with Chris Grabenstein*)
Peril at the Top of the World (*with Chris Grabenstein*)
Quest for the City of Gold (*with Chris Grabenstein*)
All-American Adventure (*with Chris Grabenstein*)
The Plunder Down Under (*with Chris Grabenstein*)
Ultimate Quest (*with Chris Grabenstein*)

DOG DIARIES SERIES
Dog Diaries (*with Steven Butler*)
Happy Howlidays! (*with Steven Butler*)
Mission Impawsible (*with Steven Butler*)
Curse of the Mystery Mutt (*with Steven Butler*)
Camping Chaos! (*with Steven Butler*)
Dinosaur Disaster! (*with Steven Butler*)
Big Top Bonanza! (*with Steven Butler*)

HOUSE OF ROBOTS SERIES
House of Robots (*with Chris Grabenstein*)
Robots Go Wild! (*with Chris Grabenstein*)
Robot Revolution (*with Chris Grabenstein*)

JACKY HA-HA SERIES
Jacky Ha-Ha (*with Chris Grabenstein*)
My Life is a Joke (*with Chris Grabenstein*)

OTHER ILLUSTRATED NOVELS
Kenny Wright: Superhero (*with Chris Tebbetts*)
Homeroom Diaries (*with Lisa Papademetriou*)
Word of Mouse (*with Chris Grabenstein*)
Pottymouth and Stoopid (*with Chris Grabenstein*)
Laugh Out Loud (*with Chris Grabenstein*)
Not So Normal Norbert (*with Joey Green*)
Unbelievably Boring Bart (*with Duane Swierczynski*)
Katt vs. Dogg (*with Chris Grabenstein*)
Scaredy Cat (*with Chris Grabenstein*)
Best Nerds Forever (*with Chris Grabenstein*)
Katt Loves Dogg (*with Chris Grabenstein*)
The Runaway's Diary (*with Emily Raymond*)

DANIEL X SERIES

The Dangerous Days of Daniel X (*with Michael Ledwidge*)
Watch the Skies (*with Ned Rust*)
Demons and Druids (*with Adam Sadler*)
Game Over (*with Ned Rust*)
Armageddon (*with Chris Grabenstein*)
Lights Out (*with Chris Grabenstein*)

For more information about James Patterson's novels,
visit www.penguin.co.uk